Goosebumps
TV Special

4

Night of the Living Dummy II

Say Cheese and Die!

Other TV Specials available:

1: The Cuckoo Clock of Doom
    The Girl Who Cried Monster

2: Welcome to Camp Nightmare
    Piano Lessons Can Be Murder

3: Return of the Mummy
    Phantom of the Auditorium

and look out for:

5: My Hairiest Adventure
    It Came From Beneath the Sink!

Goosebumps
TV Special

4

Night of the Living Dummy II
Say Cheese and Die!

R.L. Stine

Hippo

Scholastic Children's Books,
Commonwealth House, 1–19 New Oxford Street, London WC1A lNU, UK
a division of Scholastic Ltd
London ~ New York ~ Toronto ~ Sydney ~ Auckland

First published in this edition by Scholastic Ltd, 1997

Night of the Living Dummy II
First published in the USA by Scholastic Inc., 1995
First published in the UK by Scholastic Ltd, 1996
Copyright © Parachute Press, Inc., 1995
Say Cheese and Die!
First published in the USA by Scholastic Inc., 1992
First published in the UK by Scholastic Ltd, 1993
Copyright © Parachute Press, Inc., 1992

GOOSEBUMPS is a trademark of Parachute Press, Inc.

ISBN 0 590 19867 X
All rights reserved

Typeset by Contour Typesetters, Southall, London
Printed by Cox & Wyman Ltd, Reading, Berks

10 9 8 7 6 5 4 3 2 1

CONTENTS

Night of the
Living Dummy II

My name is Amy Kramer, and every Thursday night I feel a bit stupid. That's because Thursday is "Family Sharing Night" at my house.

Sara and Jed think it's stupid, too. But Mum and Dad won't listen to our complaints. "It's the most important night of the week," Dad says.

"It's a family tradition," Mum adds. "It's something you kids will always remember."

Right, Mum. It's something I'll always remember as really painful and embarrassing.

You've probably guessed that on Family Sharing Night, every member of the Kramer family—except for George, our cat—has to share something with the rest of the family.

It isn't so bad for my sister, Sara. Sara is fourteen—two years older than me—and she's a genius painter. Really. One of her paintings was chosen for a show at the art museum in town.

3

Sara may go to a special arts high school next year.

So Sara always shares some sketches she's working on. Or a new painting.

And Family Sharing Night isn't so bad for Jed, either. My ten-year-old brother is such a total goof. He doesn't care what he shares. One Thursday night, he burped really loud and explained that he was sharing his dinner.

Jed laughed like a lunatic.

But Mum and Dad didn't think it was funny. They gave Jed a stern lecture about taking Family Sharing Night more seriously.

The next Thursday night, my obnoxious brother shared a note that David Miller, a kid at my school, had written to me. A very personal note! Jed found the note in my room and decided to share it with everyone.

Nice?

I wanted to die. I really did.

Jed just thinks he's so cute and adorable, he can get away with anything. He thinks he's really special.

I think it's because he's the only redhead in the family. Sara and I both have straight black hair, dark green eyes and very dark skin. With his pale skin, freckled face and curly red hair, Jed looks as if he comes from another family!

And sometimes Sara and I both wish he did.

Anyway, I'm the one with the most problems on Family Sharing Night. Because I'm not really talented the way Sara is. And I'm not a total goof like Jed.

So I never really know what to share.

I mean, I have a seashell collection, which I keep in a jar on my dresser. But it's really quite boring to hold up shells and talk about them. And we haven't been to the ocean for nearly two years. So my shells are kind of old, and everyone has already seen them.

I also have a really good collection of CDs. But no one else in my family is into Bob Marley and reggae music. If I start to share some music with them, they all hold their ears and complain till I turn it off.

So I usually make up some kind of a story—an adventure story about a girl who survives danger after danger. Or a wild fairy tale about princesses who turn into tigers.

After my last story, Dad had a big smile on his face. "Amy is going to be a famous writer," he announced. "She's so good at making up stories." Dad gazed around the room, still smiling. "We have such a talented family!" he exclaimed.

I knew he was just saying that to be a good parent. To "encourage" me. Sara is the real talent in our family. Everyone knows that.

Tonight, Jed was the first to share. Mum and

Dad sat on the living room couch. Dad had taken out a tissue and was squinting as he cleaned his glasses. Dad can't stand to have the tiniest speck of dust on his glasses. He cleans them about twenty times a day.

I settled in the big brown armchair against the wall. Sara sat cross-legged on the carpet beside my chair.

"What are you going to share tonight?" Mum asked Jed. "And I hope it isn't another horrible burp."

"That was so disgusting!" Sara moaned.

"Your face is disgusting!" Jed shot back. He stuck out his tongue at Sara.

"Jed, please—give us a break tonight," Dad muttered, slipping his glasses back on, adjusting them on his nose. "Don't cause trouble."

"She started it," Jed insisted, pointing at Sara.

"Just share something," I told Jed, sighing.

"I'm going to share your freckles," Sara told him. "I'm going to pull them off one by one and feed them to George."

Sara and I laughed. George didn't glance up. He was curled up, napping on the carpet beside the couch.

"That's not funny, girls," Mum snapped. "Stop being mean to your brother."

"This is supposed to be a family night," Dad wailed. "Why can't we be a family?"

"We are!" Jed insisted.

Dad frowned and shook his head. He looks like an owl when he does that. "Jed, are you going to share something?" he demanded weakly.

Jed nodded. "Yeah." He stood in the centre of the room and shoved his hands into his jeans pockets. He wears loose, baggy jeans about ten sizes too big. They always look as if they're about to fall down. Jed thinks that's cool.

"I . . . uh . . . learned to whistle through my fingers," he announced.

"Wow," Sara muttered sarcastically.

Jed ignored her. He pulled his hands from his pockets. Then he stuck his two little fingers into the sides of his mouth—and let out a long, shrill whistle.

He whistled through his fingers twice more. Then he took a deep bow. The whole family burst into loud applause.

Jed, grinning, took another low bow.

"Such a talented family!" Dad declared. This time, he meant it as a joke.

Jed dropped down on the floor beside George, startling the poor cat awake.

"Your turn next, Amy," Mum said, turning to me. "Are you going to tell us another story?"

"Her stories are too long!" Jed complained.

George climbed unsteadily to his feet and moved a few feet away from Jed. Yawning, the cat dropped on to his stomach beside Mum's feet.

"I'm not going to tell a story tonight," I announced. I picked up Dennis from behind my armchair.

Sara and Jed both groaned.

"Hey—give me a break!" I shouted. I settled back on the edge of the chair, fixing my dummy on my lap. "I thought I'd talk to Dennis tonight," I told Mum and Dad.

They had half-smiles on their faces. I didn't care. I'd been practising with Dennis all week. And I wanted to try out my new comedy routine with him.

"Amy is a lousy ventriloquist," Jed chimed in. "You can see her lips move."

"Be quiet, Jed. I think Dennis is funny," Sara said. She scooted towards the couch so she could see better.

I balanced Dennis on my left knee and wrapped my fingers around the string in his back that worked his mouth. Dennis is a very old ventriloquist's dummy. The paint on his face is faded. One eye is almost completely white. His turtle-neck sweater is torn and tattered.

But I have a lot of fun with him. When my five-year-old cousins come to visit, I like to entertain them with Dennis. They squeal and laugh. They think I'm a riot.

I think I'm getting much better with Dennis. Despite Jed's complaints.

8

I took a deep breath, glanced at Mum and Dad, and began my act.

"How are you tonight, Dennis?" I asked.

"*Not too well*," I made the dummy reply in a high, shrill voice. Dennis's voice.

"Really, Dennis? What's wrong?"

"*I think I've caught a bug.*"

"You mean you have the flu?" I asked him.

"*No. Termites!*"

Mum and Dad laughed. Sara smiled. Jed groaned loudly.

I turned back to Dennis. "Well, have you been to a doctor?" I asked him.

"*No. A carpenter!*"

Mum and Dad smiled at that one, but didn't laugh. Jed groaned again. Sara stuck her finger down her throat, pretending to puke.

"No one liked that joke, Dennis," I told him.

"*Who's joking?*" I made Dennis reply.

"This is lame," I heard Jed mutter to Sara. She nodded her head in agreement.

"Let's change the subject, Dennis," I said, shifting the dummy to my other knee. "Do you have a girlfriend?"

I leaned Dennis forward, trying to make him nod his head yes. But his head rolled right off his shoulders.

The wooden head hit the floor with a *thud* and bounced over to George. The cat leaped up and scampered away.

Sara and Jed collapsed in laughter, slapping each other high fives.

I jumped angrily to my feet. "Dad!" I screamed. "You *promised* you'd buy me a new dummy!"

Jed scurried over to the rug and picked up Dennis's head. He pulled the string, making the dummy's mouth move. "Amy stinks! Amy stinks!" Jed made the dummy repeat over and over again.

"Give me that!" I grabbed the head angrily from Jed's hand.

"Amy stinks! Amy stinks!" Jed continued chanting.

"That's enough!" Mum shouted, jumping up off the couch.

Jed retreated back to the wall.

"I've been checking the shops for a new dummy," Dad told me, pulling off his glasses again and examining them closely. "But they're all so expensive."

"Well, how am I ever going to get better at this?" I demanded. "Dennis's head falls off every time I use him!"

"Do your best," Mum said.

What did *that* mean? I always hated it when she said that.

"Instead of Family Sharing Night, we should call this the Thursday Night Fights," Sara declared.

Jed raised his fists. "Want to fight?" he asked Sara.

"It's your turn, Sara," Mum replied, narrowing her eyes at Jed. "What are you sharing tonight?"

"I have a new painting," Sara announced. "It's a watercolour."

"Of what?" Dad asked, settling his glasses back on his face.

"Remember that cabin we had in Maine a few summers ago?" Sara replied, tossing back her straight black hair. "The one overlooking the dark rock cliff? I found a snapshot of it, and I tried to paint it."

I suddenly felt really angry and upset. I admit it. I was jealous of Sara.

Here she was, about to share another beautiful watercolour. And here I was, rolling a stupid wooden dummy's head in my lap.

It just wasn't fair!

"You'll have to come to my room to see it," Sara was saying. "It's still wet."

We all stood up and trooped to Sara's room.

My family lives in a long, one-storey ranch-style house. My room and Jed's room are at the end of one hallway. The living room, dining room, and kitchen are in the middle. Sara's room and my parents' room are down the other hall, way at the other end of the house.

I led the way down the hall. Behind me, Sara

11

was going on and on about all the trouble she'd had with the painting and how she'd solved the problems.

"I remember that cabin so well," Dad said.

"I can't wait to see the painting," Mum added.

I stepped into Sara's room and clicked on the light.

Then I turned to the easel by the window that held the painting—and let out a scream of horror.

My mouth dropped open in shock. I stared at the painting, unable to speak.

When Sara saw it, she let out a shriek. "I—I don't *believe* it!" she screamed. "Who *did* that?"

Someone had painted a yellow-and-black smiley face in the corner of her painting. Right in the middle of the black rock cliff.

Mum and Dad stepped up to the easel, fretful expressions on their faces. They studied the smiley face, then turned to Jed.

Jed burst out laughing. "Do you like it?" he asked innocently.

"Jed—how *could* you!" Sara exploded. "I'll kill you! I really will!"

"The painting was too dark," Jed explained with a shrug. "I wanted to brighten it up."

"But... but... but..." my sister sputtered. She clenched her hands into fists, shook them at Jed, and uttered a loud cry of rage.

13

"Jed—what were you doing in Sara's room?" Mum demanded.

Sara doesn't like anyone to go into her precious room without a written invitation!

"Young man, you know you're never allowed to touch your sister's paintings," Dad scolded.

"I can paint, too," Jed replied. "I'm a good painter."

"Then do your own paintings!" Sara snapped. "Don't sneak in here and mess up my work!"

"I didn't sneak," Jed insisted. He sneered at Sara. "I was just trying to help."

"You were not!" Sara screamed, angrily tossing her black hair over her shoulder. "You ruined my painting!"

"Your painting stinks!" Jed shot back.

"*Enough!*" Mum shouted. She grabbed Jed by both shoulders. "Jed—look at me! You don't seem to see how serious this is. This is the worst thing you've ever done!"

Jed's smile finally faded.

I took another glance at the ugly smiley face he had slopped on to Sara's watercolour. Since he's the baby in the family, Jed thinks he can get away with anything.

But I knew that this time he had gone too far.

After all, Sara is the star of the family. She's the talented one. The one with the painting that hung in a museum. Messing with Sara's precious painting was bound to get Jed in major trouble.

14

Sara is so stuck-up about her paintings. A few times, I even thought about painting something funny on one of them. But of course I only *thought* it. I would *never* do anything that horrible.

"You don't have to be jealous of your sister's work," Dad was telling Jed. "We're all talented in this family."

"Oh, sure," Jed muttered. He has this weird habit. Whenever he's in trouble, he doesn't say he's sorry. Instead, he gets really angry. "What's *your* talent, Dad?" Jed demanded, sneering.

Dad's jaw tightened. He narrowed his eyes at Jed. "We're not discussing me," he said in a low voice. "But I'll tell you. My talent is my Chinese cooking. You see, there are all kinds of talents, Jed."

Dad considers himself a Master of the Wok. Once or twice a week, he chops a ton of vegetables into little pieces and fries them up in the electric wok Mum got him for Christmas.

We pretend it tastes great.

No point in hurting Dad's feelings.

"Is Jed going to be punished or not?" Sara demanded in a shrill voice.

She had opened her box of watercolour paints and was rolling a brush in the black. Then she began painting over the smiley face with quick, furious strokes.

"Yes, Jed is going to be punished," Mum

replied, glaring at him. Jed lowered his eyes to the floor. "First he's going to apologize to Sara."

We all waited.

It took Jed a while. But he finally managed to mutter, "Sorry, Sara."

He started to leave the room, but Mum grabbed his shoulders again and pulled him back. "Not so fast, Jed," she told him. "Your punishment is you can't go to the cinema with Josh and Matt on Saturday. And . . . no video games for a week."

"Mum—give me a break!" Jed whined.

"What you did was really bad," Mum said sternly. "Maybe this punishment will make you realize how horrible it was."

"But I *have* to go to the cinema!" Jed protested.

"You can't," Mum replied softly. "And no arguing, or I'll add on to your punishment. Now go to your room."

"I don't think it's enough punishment," Sara said, dabbing away at her painting.

"Keep out of it, Sara," Mum snapped.

"Yeah. Keep out of it," Jed muttered. He stomped out of the room and down the long hall to his room.

Dad sighed. He swept a hand back over his bald head. "Family Sharing Night is over," he said sadly.

* * *

I stayed in Sara's room and watched her repair the painting for a while. She kept tsk-tsking and shaking her head.

"I have to make the rocks much darker, or the paint won't cover the stupid smiley face," she explained unhappily. "But if I make the rocks darker, I have to change the sky. The whole balance is ruined."

"I think it looks pretty good," I told her, trying to cheer her up.

"How could Jed do that?" Sara demanded, dipping her brush in the water jar. "How could he sneak in here and totally destroy a work of art?"

I was feeling sorry for Sara. But that remark made me lose all sympathy. I mean, why couldn't she just call it a watercolour painting? Why did she have to call it "a work of art"?

Sometimes she is so stuck-up and so in love with herself, it makes me sick.

I turned and left the room. She didn't even notice.

I went down the hall to my room and called my friend Margo. We talked for a while about stuff. And we made plans to get together the next day.

As I talked on the phone, I could hear Jed in his room next door. He was pacing back and forth, throwing things around, making a lot of noise.

Sometimes I spell the word "Jed" B-R-A-T.

17

Margo's dad made her get off the phone. He's really strict. He never lets her talk for more than ten or fifteen minutes.

I wandered into the kitchen and got myself a bowl of Frosted Flakes. My favourite late snack. When I was a little kid, I used to have a bowl of cereal every night before bed. And I just never got out of the habit.

I rinsed out the bowl. Then I said good night to Mum and Dad and went to bed.

It was a warm spring night. A soft breeze fluttered the curtains over the window. Pale light from a big half-moon filled the window and spilled on to the floor.

I fell into a deep sleep as soon as my head hit the pillow.

A short while later, something woke me up. I'm not sure what.

Still half asleep, I blinked my eyes open and raised myself on my pillow. I struggled to see clearly.

The curtains flapped over the window.

I felt as if I were still asleep, dreaming.

But what I saw in the window snapped me awake.

The curtains billowed, then lifted away.

And in the silvery light, I saw a face.

An ugly, grinning face in my bedroom window. Staring through the darkness at me.

18

The curtains flapped again.

The face didn't move.

"Who—?" I choked out, squeezing the sheet up to my chin.

The eyes stared in at me. Cold, unblinking eyes.

Dummy eyes.

Dennis.

Dennis stared blankly at me, his white eye catching the glow of the moonlight.

I let out an angry roar, threw off the sheet, and bolted out of bed. To the window.

I pushed away the billowing curtains and grabbed Dennis's head off the window ledge. "Who put you there?" I demanded, holding the head between my hands. "Who did it, Dennis?"

I heard soft laughter behind me. From the hallway.

I flew across the room, the head still in my hands. I pulled open my bedroom door.

19

Jed held his hand over his mouth, muffling his laughter. "Gotcha!" he whispered gleefully.

"Jed—you creep!" I cried. I let the dummy's head drop to the floor. Then I grabbed Jed's pyjama trousers with both hands and jerked them up as high as I could—nearly to his chin!

He let out a gasp of pain and stumbled back against the wall.

"Why did you do that?" I demanded in an angry whisper. "Why did you put the dummy's head on my window ledge?"

Jed tugged his pyjama trousers back into place. "To pay you back," he muttered.

"Huh? Me?" I shrieked. "I didn't do anything to you. What did *I* do?"

"You didn't stick up for me," he grumbled, scratching his red curly hair. His eyes narrowed at me. "You didn't say anything to help me out. You know. About Sara's painting."

"Excuse me?" I cried. "How could I help you out? What could I say?"

"You could have said it was no big deal," Jed replied.

"But it *was* a big deal!" I told him. "You know how seriously Sara takes her paintings." I shook my head. "I'm sorry, Jed. But you deserve to be punished. You really do."

He stared at me across the dim hallway, thinking about what I'd said. Then an evil smile spread slowly over his freckled face. "Hope I didn't scare you too much, Amy." He sniggered. Then he picked Dennis's head up off the carpet and threw it at me.

I caught it in one hand. "Go to sleep, Jed," I told him. "And don't mess with Dennis again!"

I stopped back into my room and closed the door. I tossed Dennis's head on to a pile of clothes on my desk chair. Then I climbed wearily back into bed.

So much trouble around here tonight, I thought, shutting my eyes, trying to relax.

So much trouble . . .

The next day, Dad brought home a present for me.

A new ventriloquist's dummy.

That's when the *real* trouble began.

Margo came over the next afternoon. Margo is really tiny, sort of like a mini-person. She has a tiny face, and is very pretty, with bright blue eyes, and delicate features.

Her blonde hair is very light and very fine. She let it grow this year. It's just about down to her tiny little waist.

She's nearly a foot shorter than me, even though we both turned twelve in February. She's very smart and very popular. But the boys like to make fun of her soft, whispery voice.

Today she was wearing a bright blue tank top tucked into white tennis shorts. "I bought the new Beatles collection," she told me as she stepped into the house. She held up a CD box.

Margo loves the Beatles. She doesn't listen to any of the new groups. In her room, she has an entire shelf of Beatles CDs and tapes. And she has Beatles posters on her walls.

We went to my room and put on the CD. Margo

settled on the bed. I sprawled on the carpet across from her.

"My dad almost didn't let me come over," Margo told me, pushing her long hair behind her shoulder. "He thought he might need me to work at the restaurant."

Margo's dad owns a huge restaurant in town called The Party House. It's not really a restaurant. It's a big, old house filled with enormous rooms where people can hold parties.

A lot of kids have birthday parties there. And there are bar mitzvahs and confirmations and wedding receptions there, too. Sometimes there are six parties going on at once!

One Beatles song ended. The next song, "Love Me Do", started up.

"I *love* this song!" Margo exclaimed. She sang along with it for a while. I tried singing with her, but I'm totally tone deaf. As my dad says, I can't carry a tune in a wheelbarrow.

"Well, I'm glad you didn't have to work today," I told Margo.

"Me, too," Margo sighed. "Dad always gives me the worst jobs. You know. Clearing tables. Or putting away dishes. Or wrapping up rubbish bags. Yuck."

She started singing again—and then stopped. She sat up on the bed. "Amy, I almost forgot. Dad may have a job for you."

"Excuse me?" I replied. "Wrapping up rubbish bags? I don't think so, Margo."

"No. No. Listen," Margo pleaded excitedly in her mouselike voice. "It's a good job. Dad has a bunch of birthday parties coming up. For teeny tiny kids. You know. Two-year-olds. Maybe three- or four-year-olds. And he thought you could entertain them."

"Huh?" I stared at my friend. I still didn't understand. "You mean, sing or something?"

"No. With Dennis," Margo explained. She twisted a lock of hair around in her fingers and bobbed her head in time to the music as she talked. "Dad saw you with Dennis at the sixth-grade talent night. He was really impressed."

"He was? I was terrible that night!" I replied.

"Well, Dad didn't think so. He wonders if you'd like to come to the birthday parties and put on a show with Dennis. The little kids will love it. Dad said he'd even pay you."

"Wow! That's cool!" I replied. What an exciting idea.

Then I remembered something.

I jumped to my feet, crossed the room to the chair, and held up Dennis's head. "One small problem," I groaned.

Margo let go of her hair and made a sick face. "His head? Why did you take off his head?"

"I didn't," I replied. "It fell off. Every time I use Dennis, his head falls off."

24

"Oh." Margo uttered a disappointed sigh. "The head looks weird all by itself. I don't think little kids would like it if it fell off."

"I don't think so," I agreed.

"It might frighten them or something," Margo said. "You know. Give them nightmares. Make them think their own head might fall off."

"Dennis is totally wrecked. Dad promised me a new dummy. But he hasn't been able to find one."

"Too bad," Margo replied. "You'd have fun performing for the kids."

We listened to more Beatles music. Then Margo had to go home.

A few minutes after she left, I heard the front door slam.

"Hey, Amy! Amy—are you home?" I heard Dad call from the living room.

"Coming!" I called. I made my way to the front of the house. Dad stood in the entryway, a long box under his arm, a smile on his face.

He handed the box to me. "Happy Unbirthday!" he exclaimed.

"Dad! Is it—?" I cried. I tore open the box. "Yes!" A new dummy!

I lifted him carefully out of the box.

The dummy had wavy brown hair painted on top of his wooden head. I studied his face. It was kind of strange. Kind of intense. His eyes were bright blue—not faded like Dennis's. He had bright red painted lips, curved up into an eerie smile. His lower lip had a chip on one side so that it didn't quite match the other lip.

As I pulled him from the box, the dummy appeared to stare into my eyes. The eyes sparkled. The grin grew wider.

I felt a sudden chill. Why does this dummy seem to be laughing at me? I wondered.

I held him up, examining him carefully. He wore a grey, double-breasted suit over a white shirt collar. The collar was stapled to his neck. He didn't have a shirt. Instead, his wooden chest had been painted white.

Big, black leather shoes were attached to the ends of his thin, dangling legs.

"Dad—he's great!" I exclaimed.

"I found him in a pawnshop," Dad said, picking up the dummy's hand and pretending to shake hands with it. "How do you do, Slappy."

"Slappy? Is that his name?"

"That's what the man in the shop said," Dad replied. He lifted Slappy's arms, examining his suit. "I don't know why he sold Slappy so cheaply. He practically *gave* the dummy away!"

I turned the dummy around and looked for the string in his back that made the mouth open and close. "He's excellent, Dad," I said. I kissed my dad on the cheek. "Thanks."

"Do you really like him?" Dad asked.

Slappy grinned up at me. His blue eyes stared

26

into mine. He seemed to be waiting for an answer, too.

"Yes. He's awesome!" I said. "I like his serious eyes. They look so real."

"The eyes move," Dad said. "They're not painted on like Dennis's. They don't blink, but they move from side to side."

I reached my hand inside the dummy's back. "How do you make his eyes move?" I asked.

"The man showed me," Dad said. "It's not hard. First you grab the string that works the mouth."

"I've got that," I told him.

"Then you move your hand up into the dummy's head. There is a little lever up there. Do you feel it? Push on it. The eyes will move in the direction you push."

"Okay. I'll try," I said.

Slowly I moved my hand up inside the dummy's back. Through the neck. And into his head.

I stopped and let out a startled cry as my hand hit something soft.

Something soft and warm.

His brain!

27

"Ohhh." I uttered a sick moan and jerked my hand out as fast as I could.

I could still feel the soft, warm mush on my fingers.

"Amy—what's wrong?" Dad cried.

"His—his brains—!" I choked out, feeling my stomach lurch.

"Huh? What are you *talking* about?" Dad grabbed the dummy from my hands. He turned it over and reached into the back.

I covered my mouth with both hands and watched him reach into the head. His eyes widened in surprise.

He struggled with something. Then pulled his hand out.

"Yuck!" I groaned. "What's *that?*"

Dad stared down at the mushy, green and purple and brown object in his hands. "Looks like someone left a sandwich in there!" he exclaimed.

Dad's whole face twisted in disgust. "It's all mouldy and rotten. Must have been in there for months!"

"Yuck!" I repeated, holding my nose. "It really stinks! Why would someone leave a sandwich in a dummy's head?"

"Beats me," Dad replied, shaking his head. "And it looks like there are wormholes in it!"

"Yuuuuuck!" we both cried in unison.

Dad handed Slappy back to me. Then he hurried into the kitchen to get rid of the rotten, mouldy sandwich.

I heard him run the waste disposal unit. Then I heard water running as he washed his hands. A few seconds later, Dad returned to the living room, drying his hands on a dish cloth.

"Maybe we'd better examine Slappy closely," he suggested. "We don't want any more surprises—*do* we!"

I carried Slappy into the kitchen, and we stretched him out on the counter. Dad examined the dummy's shoes carefully. They were attached to the legs and didn't come off.

I put my finger on the dummy's chin and moved the mouth up and down. Then I checked out his wooden hands.

I unbuttoned the grey suit jacket and studied the dummy's painted shirt. Patches of the white paint had chipped and cracked. But it was okay.

"Everything looks fine, Dad," I reported.

He nodded. Then he smelled his fingers. I guess he hadn't washed away all of the stink from the rotten sandwich.

"We'd better spray the inside of his head with disinfectant or perfume or something," Dad said.

Then, as I was buttoning up the jacket, something caught my eye.

Something yellow. A slip of paper poking up from the jacket pocket.

It's probably a sales receipt, I thought.

But when I pulled out the small square of yellow paper, I found strange writing on it. Weird words in a language I'd never seen before.

I squinted hard at the paper and slowly read the words out loud:

"Karru marri odonna loma molonu karrano."

I wonder what that means? I thought.

And then I glanced down at Slappy's face.

And saw his red lips twitch.

And saw one eye slowly close in a wink.

"D-d-dad!" I stuttered. "He—moved!"

"Huh?" Dad had gone back to the sink to wash his hands for a third time. "What's wrong with the dummy?"

"He moved!" I cried. "He *winked* at me!"

Dad came over to the counter, wiping his hands. "I told you, Amy—he can't blink. The eyes only move from side to side."

"No!" I insisted. "He winked. His lips twitch-ed, and he winked."

Dad frowned and picked up the dummy's head in both hands. He raised it to examine it. "Well ... maybe the eyelids are loose," he said. "I'll see if I can tighten them up. Maybe if I take a screwdriver I can—"

Dad didn't finish his sentence.

Because the dummy swung his wooden hand up and hit Dad on the side of the head.

"Ow!" Dad cried, dropping the dummy back on to the counter. Dad grabbed his cheek.

"Hey—stop it, Amy! That hurt!"

"*Me?*" I shrieked. "I didn't do it!"

Dad glared at me, rubbing his cheek. It had turned bright red.

"The dummy did it!" I insisted. "I didn't touch him, Dad! I didn't move his hand!"

"Not funny," Dad muttered. "You know I don't like practical jokes."

I opened my mouth to answer, but no words came out. I decided I'd better just shut up.

Of course Dad wouldn't believe that the dummy had slapped him.

I didn't believe it myself.

Dad must have pulled too hard when he was examining the head. Dad jerked the hand up without realizing it.

That's how I explained it to myself.

What other explanation could there be?

I apologized to Dad. Then we washed Slappy's face with a damp sponge. We cleaned him up and sprayed disinfectant inside his head.

He was starting to look pretty good.

I thanked Dad again and hurried to my room. I set Slappy down on the chair beside Dennis. Then I phoned Margo.

"I've got a new dummy," I told her excitedly. "I can perform for the kids' birthday parties. At The Party House."

"That's great, Amy!" Margo exclaimed.

"Now all you need is an act."

She was right.

I needed jokes. A lot of jokes. If I was going to perform with Slappy in front of dozens of kids, I needed a long comedy act.

The next day after school, I hurried to the library. I took out every joke book I could find. I carried them home and studied them. I wrote down all the jokes I thought I could use with Slappy.

After dinner, I should have been doing my homework. Instead, I practised with Slappy. I sat in front of the mirror and watched myself with him.

I tried hard to speak clearly but not move my lips. And I tried hard to move Slappy's mouth so that it really looked as if he were talking.

Working his mouth and moving his eyes at the same time was pretty hard. But after a while, it became easier.

I tried some knock-knock jokes with Slappy. I thought little kids might like those.

"Knock knock," I made Slappy say.

"Who's there?" I asked him, staring into his eyes as if I were really talking to him.

"Jane," Slappy said.

"Jane who?"

"Jane jer clothes. You stink!"

I practised each joke over and over, watching myself in the mirror. I wanted to be a really good ventriloquist. I wanted to be excellent. I wanted to be as good with Slappy as Sara is with her paints.

I practised some more knock-knock jokes and some jokes about animals. Jokes I thought little kids would find funny.

I'll try them out on Family Sharing Night, I decided. It will make Dad happy to see how hard I'm working with Slappy. At least I know Slappy's head won't fall off.

I glanced across the room at Dennis. He looked so sad and forlorn, crumpled in the chair, his head tilted nearly sideways on his shoulders.

Then I propped Slappy up and turned back to the mirror.

"Knock knock."

"Who's there?"

"Wayne."

"Wayne who?"

"Wayne wayne, go away! Come again another day!"

On Thursday night, I was actually eager to finish dinner so that Sharing Night could begin. I couldn't wait to show my family my new act with Slappy.

We had spaghetti for dinner. I like spaghetti, but Jed always ruins it.

He's so gross. He sat across the table from me, and he kept opening his mouth wide, showing

34

me a mouth full of chewed-up spaghetti.

Then he'd laugh because he cracks himself up. And spaghetti sauce would run down his chin.

By the time dinner was over, Jed had spaghetti sauce smeared all over his face and all over the tablecloth around his plate.

No one seemed to notice. Mum and Dad were too busy listening to Sara brag about her grades. For a change.

Report cards were being handed out tomorrow. Sara was sure she was getting all A's.

I was sure, too. Sure I *wasn't* getting all A's!

I'd be lucky to get a C for maths. I really messed up the last two tests. And I probably wasn't going to do all that well in science, either. My weather balloon project fell apart, so I hadn't handed it in yet.

I finished my spaghetti and mopped up some of the leftover sauce on my plate with a chunk of bread.

When I glanced up, Jed had stuck two carrot sticks in his nose. "Amy, check this out. I'm a walrus!" he cried, grinning. He let out a few *urk urks* and clapped his hands together like a walrus.

"Jed—stop that!" Mum cried sharply. She made a disgusted face. "Get those out of your nose."

"Make him eat them, Mum!" I cried.

Jed stuck his tongue out at me. It was orange from the spaghetti sauce.

"Look at you. You're a mess!" Mum shouted at Jed. "Go and get cleaned up. Now! Hurry! Wash all that sauce off your face."

Jed groaned. But he climbed to his feet and headed to the bathroom.

"Did he eat anything? Or did he just rub it all over himself?" Dad asked, rolling his eyes. Dad had some sauce on his chin, too, but I didn't say anything.

"You interrupted me," Sara said impatiently. "I was telling you about the State Art Contest. Remember? I sent my flower painting in for that?"

"Oh, yes," Mum replied. "Have you heard from the judges?"

I didn't listen to Sara's reply. My mind wandered. I started thinking again about how bad my report was going to be. I had to force myself to stop thinking about it.

"Uh . . . I'll clear the dishes," I announced.

I started to stand up.

But I stopped with a startled cry when I saw the short figure creep into the living room.

A dummy!

My dummy.

He was crawling across the room!

I let out another cry. I pointed to the living room with a trembling finger. "M-mum! Dad!" I stammered.

Sara was still talking about the art competition. But she turned to see what everyone was gaping at.

The dummy's head popped out from behind the armchair.

"It's Dennis!" I cried.

I heard muffled laughter. Jed's muffled laughter.

The dummy reached up both hands and pulled off his own head. And Jed's head popped up through the green turtleneck. He still had spaghetti sauce smeared on his cheeks. He was laughing hard.

Everyone else started to laugh, too. Everyone but me.

Jed had really frightened me.

He had pulled the neck of his sweater way up

37

over his head. Then he had tucked Dennis's wooden head inside the turtleneck.

Jed was so short and thin. It really looked as if Dennis were creeping into the room.

"Stop laughing!" I shouted at my family. "It isn't funny!"

"I think it's *very* funny!" Mum cried. "What a crazy thing to think of!"

"Very clever," Dad added.

"It's not clever," I insisted. I glared furiously at my brother. "I always knew you were a dummy!" I screamed at him.

"Amy, you really were scared," Sara accused. "You nearly dropped your teeth!"

"Not true!" I sputtered. "I knew it was Dennis—I mean—Jed!"

Now everyone started laughing at *me*! I could feel my face getting hot, and I knew I was blushing.

That made them all laugh even harder.

Nice family, huh?

I climbed to my feet, walked around the table, and took Dennis's head away from Jed. "Don't go in my room," I told him through clenched teeth. "And don't mess with my stuff." I stomped away to put the dummy's head back in my room.

"It was just a joke, Amy," I heard Sara call after me.

"Yeah. It was just a joke," Jed repeated nastily.

"Ha-ha!" I shouted back at them. "What a riot!"

My anger had faded away by the time we started Family Sharing Night. We settled in the living room, taking our usual places.

Mum volunteered to go first. She told a funny story about something that had happened at work.

Mum works in a fancy women's clothing store in town. She told us about a really big woman who came into the store and insisted on trying on only tiny sizes.

The woman ripped every piece of clothing she tried on—and then bought them all! "They're not for me," the woman explained. "They're for my sister!"

We all laughed. But I was surprised Mum told that story. Because Mum is pretty chubby. And she's very sensitive about it.

About as sensitive as Dad is about being bald.

Dad was the next to share. He brought out his guitar, and we all groaned. Dad thinks he's a great singer. But he's nearly as tone deaf as I am.

He loves singing all these old folk songs from the sixties. There's supposed to be some kind of message in them. But Sara, Jed and I have no idea what he's singing about.

Dad strummed away and sang something

about not working on Maggie's farm any more. At least, I *think* that's what he was saying.

We all clapped and cheered. But Dad knew we didn't really mean it.

It was Jed's turn next. But he insisted that he had already shared. "Dressing up like Dennis—that was it," he said.

No one wanted to argue with him. "Your turn, Amy," Mum said, leaning against Dad on the couch. Dad fiddled with his glasses, then settled back.

I picked up Slappy and arranged him on my lap. I was feeling a little nervous. I wanted to do a good job and impress them with my new comedy act.

I'd been practising all week, and I knew the jokes by heart. But as I slipped my hand into Slappy's back and found the string, my stomach felt all fluttery.

I cleared my throat and began.

"This is Slappy, everyone," I said. "Slappy, say hi to my family."

"*Hi to my family!*" I made Slappy say. I made his eyes slide back and forth.

They all chuckled.

"This dummy is much better!" Mum commented.

"But it's the same old ventriloquist," Sara said cruelly.

I glared at her.

"Just joking! Just joking!" my sister insisted.

"I think that dummy stinks," Jed chimed in.

"Give Amy a break," Dad said sharply. "Go ahead, Amy."

I cleared my throat again. It suddenly felt very dry. "Slappy and I are going to tell some knock-knock jokes," I announced. I turned to face Slappy and made him turn his head to me. "Knock-knock," I said.

"*Knock it off!*" came the harsh reply.

Slappy spun around to face my mum. "*Hey— don't break the sofa, fatso!*" he rasped. "*Why don't you skip the French fries and have a salad once in a while?*"

"Huh?" Mum gasped in shock. "Amy—"

"Amy, that's not funny!" Dad cried angrily.

"*What's your problem, baldy?*" Slappy shouted. "*Is that your head—or are you hatching an ostrich egg on your neck?*"

"That's enough, Amy!" Dad cried, jumping to his feet. "Stop it—right now!"

"But—but—Dad!" I sputtered.

"*Why don't you put an extra hole in your head and use it for a bowling ball?*" Slappy screamed at Dad.

"Your jokes are horrible!" Mum exclaimed. "They're hurtful and insulting."

"It's not funny, Amy!" Dad fumed. "It's not funny to hurt people's feelings."

41

"But, Dad—" I replied. "I didn't say any of that! It wasn't me! It was Slappy! Really! I wasn't saying it! I wasn't!"

Slappy raised his head. His red-lipped grin appeared to spread. His blue eyes sparkled. "*Did I mention you are all ugly?*" he asked.

Everyone started shouting at once.

I stood up and dropped Slappy face down on the armchair.

My legs were trembling. My entire body was shaking.

What's going on here? I asked myself. I didn't say those things. I really didn't.

But Slappy can't be talking on his own—*can he*?

Of course not, I realized.

But what did that mean? Did that mean I was saying those horrible, insulting things to my parents without even knowing it?

Mum and Dad stood side by side, staring at me angrily, demanding to know why I had insulted them.

"Did you really think that was funny?" Mum asked. "Didn't you think it would hurt my feelings to call me fatso?"

Meanwhile, Jed was sprawled on his back in

43

the middle of the floor, giggling like a moron. He thought the whole thing was a riot.

Sara sat cross-legged against the wall, shaking her head, her black hair falling over her face. "You're in major trouble," she muttered. "What's your problem, Amy?"

I turned to Mum and Dad. My hands were clenched into tight fists. I couldn't stop shaking.

"You've got to believe me!" I shrieked. "I didn't say those things! I really didn't!"

"Yeah. Right. Slappy is a baaad dude!" Jed chimed in, grinning.

"Everybody, just be quiet!" Dad screamed. His face turned bright red.

Mum squeezed his arm. She didn't like it when he got too angry or excited. I guess she worried he might totally explode or something.

Dad crossed his arms in front of his chest. I saw that he had a sweat stain on the chest of his polo shirt. His face was still red.

The room suddenly fell silent.

"Amy, we're *not* going to believe you," Dad said softly.

"But—but—but—"

He raised a hand to silence me.

"You're a wonderful storyteller, Amy," Dad continued. "You make up wonderful fantasies and fairy tales. But we're not going to believe this one. I'm sorry. We're not going to believe that your dummy spoke up on his own."

44

"But he *did*!" I screamed. I felt like bursting out in sobs. I bit my lip hard, trying to force them back.

Dad shook his head. "No, Slappy didn't insult us. You said those things, Amy. You did. And now I want you to apologize to your mother and me. Then I want you to take your dummy and go to your room."

There was no way they'd ever believe me. No way. I wasn't sure I believed it myself.

"Sorry," I muttered, still holding back the tears. "Really. I'm sorry."

With an unhappy sigh, I lifted Slappy off the chair. I carried him around the waist so that his arms and legs dangled towards the floor. "Good night," I said. I walked slowly towards my room.

"What about my turn?" I heard Sara ask.

"Sharing Night is over," Dad replied grumpily. "You two—get lost. Leave your mum and me alone."

Dad sounded really upset.

I didn't blame him.

I stepped into my room and closed the door behind me. Then I lifted Slappy up, holding him under the shoulders. I raised his face to mine.

His eyes seemed to stare into my face.

Such cold blue eyes, I thought.

His bright red lips curled up into that smirking grin. The smile suddenly seemed evil. Mocking.

As if Slappy were laughing at me.

But of course that was impossible. My wild imagination was playing tricks on me, I decided.

Frightening tricks.

Slappy was just a dummy, after all. Just a hunk of painted wood.

I stared hard into those cold blue eyes. "Slappy, look at all the trouble you caused me tonight," I told him.

Thursday night had been awful. Totally awful.

But Friday turned out to be much worse.

First I dropped my tray in the canteen. The trays were all wet, and mine just slipped out of my hand.

The plates clattered on the floor, and my lunch spilled all over my new white trainers. Everyone in the canteen clapped and cheered.

Was I embarrassed? Take three guesses.

Later that afternoon, report cards were handed out.

Sara came home grinning and singing. Nothing makes her more happy than being perfect. And her report card was perfect. All A's.

She insisted on showing it to me three times. She showed it to Jed three times, too. And we both had to tell her how wonderful she was each time.

I'm being unfair to Sara.

She was happy and excited. And she had a right to be. Her report card was perfect—*and* her flower painting won the blue ribbon in the State Art Contest.

So I shouldn't blame her for dancing around the house and singing at the top of her lungs.

She wasn't trying to rub it in. She wasn't trying to make me feel like a lowly slug because my report card had two C's. One for maths and one for science.

It wasn't Sara's fault that I had received my worst report card ever.

So I tried to hold back my jealous feelings and not strangle her the tenth time she told me about the art prize. But it wasn't easy.

The worst part of my report card wasn't the two C's. It was the little note Miss Carson wrote at the bottom.

It said: *Amy isn't working to the best of her ability. If she worked harder, she could do much better than this.*

I don't think teachers should be allowed to write notes on report cards. I think getting grades is bad enough.

I tried to make up some kind of story to explain the two C's to my parents. I planned to tell them that *everyone* in the class got C's for maths and science. "Miss Carson didn't have time to grade our papers. So she gave us all C's—just to be fair."

It was a good story. But not a great story.

No way Mum and Dad would buy that one.

I paced back and forth in my room, trying to think of a better story. After a while, I noticed Slappy staring at me.

He sat in the chair beside Dennis, grinning and staring.

Slappy's eyes weren't following me as I paced—were they?

I felt a chill run down my back.

It really seemed as if the eyes were watching me, moving as I moved.

I darted to the chair and turned Slappy so that his back was to me. I didn't have time to think about a stupid dummy. My parents would be home from work any minute. And I needed a good story to explain my awful report card.

Did I come up with one? No.

Were my parents upset? Yes.

Mum said she would help me get better organized. Dad said he would help me understand my maths problems. The last time Dad helped me with my maths, I nearly failed!

Even Jed—the total goof-off—got a better report card than me. They don't give grades in the lower school. The teacher just writes a report about you.

And Jed's report said that he was a great kid and a really good student. That teacher must be *sick*!

I stared at Jed across the dinner table. He

opened his mouth wide to show me a mouth full of chewed-up peas.

Sick!

"You stink," he said to me. For no reason at all.

Sometimes I wonder why families were invented.

Saturday morning, I called Margo. "I can't come over," I told her with a sigh. "My parents won't let me."

"My report card wasn't too good, either," Margo replied. "Miss Carson wrote a note at the bottom. She said I talk too much in class."

"Miss Carson talks too much," I said bitterly.

As I chatted with Margo, I stared at myself in the dresser mirror. I look too much like Sara, I thought. Why do I have to look like her twin? Maybe I'll cut my hair really short. Or get a tattoo.

I wasn't thinking too clearly.

I was too angry that my parents weren't allowing me to go over to Margo's house.

"This is bad news," Margo said. "I wanted to talk to you about performing with Slappy at my dad's place."

"I know," I replied sadly. "But they're not letting me go anywhere until my science project is finished."

"You still haven't handed that in?" Margo demanded.

"I kind of forgot about it," I confessed. "I did the project part—for the second time. I just have to write the report."

"Well, I told you, Daddy has a birthday party for a dozen three-year-olds next Saturday," Margo said. "And he wants you and Slappy to entertain them."

"As soon as I finish the science report, I'm going to start rehearsing," I promised. "Tell your dad not to worry, Margo. Tell him I'll be great."

We chatted for a few more minutes. Then my mum shouted for me to get off the phone. I talked for a little while longer—until Mum shouted a second time. Then I said goodbye to Margo and hung up.

I slaved over my computer all morning and most of the afternoon. And I finished the science report.

It wasn't easy. Jed kept coming into my room, begging me to play a Nintendo game with him. "Just one!" And I had to keep throwing him out.

When I finally finished writing the paper, I printed it out and read it one more time. I thought it was pretty good.

What it needs is a really great-looking cover, I decided.

I wanted to get a bunch of coloured pens and

do a really bright cover. But my felt-tips were all dried up.

I tossed them into the bin and made my way to Sara's room. I knew that she had an entire drawer filled with felt-tips.

Sara was at the shops with a bunch of her friends. Miss Perfect could go out and spend Saturday doing whatever she wanted. Because she was perfect.

I knew she wouldn't mind if I borrowed a few pens.

Jed stopped me outside her door. "One game of Battle Chess!" he pleaded. "Just one game!"

"No way," I told him. I placed my hand on top of his head. His red, curly hair felt so soft. I pushed him out of my way. "You always murder me at Battle Chess. And I'm not finished with my work yet."

"Why are you going in Sara's room?" he demanded.

"None of your business," I told him.

"You stink," he said. "You double stink, Amy."

I ignored him and made my way into Sara's room to borrow the felt-tips.

I spent nearly an hour making the cover. I filled it with molecules and atoms, all in different colours. Miss Carson will be impressed, I decided.

Sara returned home just as I finished. She was

carrying a big shopping bag filled with clothes she'd bought at Banana Republic.

She started to her room with the bag. "Mum—come and see what I bought," she called.

Mum appeared, carrying a stack of freshly laundered towels.

"Can I see, too?" I called. I followed them to Sara's room.

But Sara stopped at her door.

The bag fell from her hand.

And she let out a scream.

Mum and I crowded behind her. We peered into the bedroom.

What a mess!

Someone had overturned about a dozen jars of paint. Reds, yellows, blues. The paint had spread over Sara's white carpet, like a big, colourful mud puddle.

I gasped and blinked several times. It was unreal!

"I don't believe it!" Sara kept shrieking. "I don't believe it!"

"The carpet is ruined!" Mum exclaimed, taking one step into the room.

The emptied paint jars were on their sides, strewn around the room.

"Jed!" Mum shouted angrily. "Jed—get in here! Now!"

We turned to see Jed right behind us in the hall. "You don't have to shout," he said softly.

Mum narrowed her eyes angrily at my brother. "Jed—how *could* you?" she demanded through clenched teeth.

"Excuse me?" He gazed up at her innocently.

"Jed—don't lie!" Sara screamed. "Did you do this? Did you go in my room again?"

"No way!" Jed protested, shaking his head. "I didn't go in your room today, Sara. Not once. But I saw Amy go in. And she wouldn't tell me why."

Sara and Mum both turned accusing eyes on me.

"How could you?" Sara screamed, walking around the big paint puddle. "How *could* you?"

"Whoa! Wait! I didn't! I didn't!" I cried frantically.

"I asked Amy why she was going in here," Jed chimed in. "And she said it was none of my business."

"Amy!" Mum cried. "I'm horrified. I'm truly horrified. This—this is *sick*!"

"Yes, it's sick," Sara repeated, shaking her head. "All of my poster paint. All of it. What a mess. I know why you did it. It's because you're jealous of my perfect report card."

"*But I didn't do it!*" I wailed. "I didn't! I didn't! I didn't!"

"Amy—no one else could have," Mum replied. "If Jed didn't do it, then—"

"But I only came in here to borrow some pens!"

55

I cried in a trembling voice. "That's all. I needed some pens."

"Amy—" Mum started, pointing to the huge paint puddle.

"I'll show you!" I cried. "I'll show you what I borrowed."

I ran to my room. My hands were shaking as I scooped Sara's felt-tips off my desk. My heart pounded.

How could they accuse me of something so terrible? I asked myself.

Is that what everyone thinks of me? That I'm such a monster?

That I'm so jealous of my sister, I'd pour out all her paints and ruin her carpet?

Do they really think I'm crazy?

I ran back to Sara's room, carrying the pens in both hands. Jed sat on Sara's bed, staring down at the thick red, blue and yellow puddle.

Mum and Sara stood over it, gazing down and shaking their heads. Mum kept making clucking noises with her tongue. She kept pressing her hands against her cheeks.

"Here! See?" I cried. I shoved the felt-tips towards them. "That's why I came in here. I'm not lying!"

Some of the pens fell out of my hands. I bent to pick them up.

"Amy, there were only three of us home this afternoon," Mum said. She was trying to keep

56

her voice low and calm. But she spoke through gritted teeth. "You, me and Jed."

"I know—" I started.

Mum raised a hand to silence me. "I certainly didn't do this horrible thing," Mum continued. "And Jed says that he didn't do it. So . . ." Her voice trailed off.

"Mum—I'm not a sicko!" I shrieked. "I'm not!"

"You'll feel better if you confess," Mum said. "Then we can talk about this calmly, and—"

"*But I didn't do it!*" I raged.

With a cry of anger, I flung the felt-tips to the floor. Then I spun around, bolted from Sara's room, and ran down the long hall to my room.

I slammed the door and threw myself face down on to my bed. I started sobbing loudly. I don't know how long I cried.

Finally, I stood up. My face was sopping wet, and my nose was running. I started to the dresser to get a tissue.

But something caught my eye.

Hadn't I turned Slappy around so that his back was turned to me?

Now he was sitting facing me, staring up at me, his red-lipped grin wider than ever.

Did I turn him back around? Did I?

I didn't remember.

And what did I see on Slappy's shoes?

I wiped the tears from my eyes with the backs of my hands. Then I took a few steps towards the dummy, squinting hard at his big leather shoes.

What *was* that on his shoes?

Red and blue and yellow . . . paint?

Yes.

With a startled gasp, I grabbed both shoes by the heels and raised them close to my face.

Yes.

Drips of paint on Slappy's shoes.

"Slappy—what is going on here?" I asked out loud. "What is going on?"

When Dad came home and saw Sara's room, he nearly exploded.

I was actually worried about him. His face turned as red as a tomato. His chest started heaving in and out. And horrible gurgling noises came up from his throat.

The whole family gathered in the living room. We took our Sharing Night places. Only, this wasn't Family Sharing Night. This was What Are We Going To Do About Amy Night.

"Amy, first you have to tell us the truth," Mum said. She sat stiffly on the couch, squeezing her hands together in her lap.

Dad sat on the other end of the couch, tapping one hand nervously against the couch arm, chewing his lower lip. Jed and Sara sat on the floor against the wall.

"I *am* telling the truth," I insisted shrilly. I slumped in the armchair across from them. My hair fell over my forehead, but I didn't bother to

59

brush it back. My white T-shirt had tear stains on the front, still damp. "If you would only listen to me," I pleaded.

"Okay, we're listening," Mum replied.

"When I went into my room," I started, "there were splashes of paint on Slappy's shoes. And—"

"Enough!" Dad cried, jumping to his feet.

"But, Dad—" I protested.

"Enough!" he insisted. He pointed a finger at me. "No more wild stories, young lady. Storytime is over. We don't want to hear about paint stains on Slappy. We want an explanation for the crime that was committed in Sara's room today."

"But I *am* giving an explanation!" I wailed. "Why did Slappy have paint on his shoes? Why?"

Dad dropped back on to the couch with a sigh. He whispered something to Mum. She whispered back.

I thought I heard them mention the word "doctor."

"Are you—are you going to take me to a psychiatrist?" I asked timidly.

"Do you think you need one?" Mum replied, staring hard at me.

I shook my head. "No."

"Your father and I will talk about this,"

Mum said. "We will figure out the best thing to do."

The best thing to do?

They grounded me for two weeks. No films. No friends over. No trips to the shops. No trips anywhere.

I heard them talking about finding me a counsellor. But they didn't say anything about it to me.

All week, I could feel them watching me. Studying me as if I were some kind of alien creature.

Sara was pretty cold to me. Her room had to be emptied out and a new carpet installed. She wasn't happy about it.

Even Jed treated me differently. He kind of tiptoed around me and kept his distance, as if I had a bad cold or something. He didn't tease me, or tell me that I stank, or call me names.

I really missed it. No kidding.

How did I feel? I felt miserable.

I wanted to get ill. I wanted to catch a really bad stomach flu or something so they'd all feel sorry for me and stop treating me like a criminal.

One good thing: they said I could perform with Slappy at The Party House on Saturday.

Whenever I picked Slappy up, I felt a little weird. I remembered the paint on his shoes and the mess in my sister's room.

But I couldn't come up with one single explanation. So I practised with Slappy every night.

I had put a lot of good jokes together. Silly jokes I thought little three-year-olds would find funny.

And I studied myself in the mirror. I was getting better at not moving my lips. And it was getting easier to make Slappy's mouth and eyes move correctly.

"Knock knock," I made Slappy say.

"Who's there?" I asked.

"Eddie."

"Eddie who?" I asked.

"Eddie-body got a tissue? I hab a teddible cold!"

And then I pulled back Slappy's head, opened his mouth really wide, and jerked his whole body as I made him sneeze and sneeze and sneeze.

I thought that would really crack up the three-year-olds.

Every night, I worked and worked on our comedy act. I worked so hard.

I didn't know that the act would never go on.

On Saturday afternoon, Mum dropped me off at The Party House. "Have a good show!" she called as she drove away.

I carried Slappy carefully in my arms. Margo

62

met me at the door. She greeted me with an excited smile.

"Just in time!" she cried. "The kids are almost all here. They're total animals!"

"Oh, great!" I muttered, rolling my eyes.

"They're total animals, but they're so cute!" Margo added.

She led me through the twisting hallway to the party room at the back. Clusters of red and yellow balloons covered the ceiling. I saw a brightly decorated table, all yellow and red. A balloon on a string floated up from each chair around the table. Each balloon had the name of a guest on it.

The kids really were cute. They were dressed mostly in jeans and bright T-shirts. Two of the girls wore frilly party dresses.

I counted ten of them, all running wildly, chasing each other in the huge room.

Their mothers were grouped around a long table against the back wall. Some of them were sitting down. Some were standing, huddled together, chatting. Some were calling to their kids to stop being so wild.

"I'm helping out, pouring the punch and stuff," Margo told me. "Dad wants you to do your act first thing. You know. To quieten the kids down."

I swallowed hard. "First thing, huh?"

I had been excited. I could barely choke down

my tuna fish sandwich at lunch. But now I began to feel nervous. I had major fluttering in my stomach.

Margo led me to the front of the room. I saw a low wooden platform there, painted bright blue. That was the stage.

Seeing the stage made my heart start to pound. My mouth suddenly felt very dry.

Could I really step up on that stage and do my act in front of all these people? Kids and mothers?

I had forgotten that the mothers would all be there. Seeing adults in the audience made me even more nervous.

"Here is the birthday girl," a woman's voice said.

I turned to see a smiling mother. She held the hand of a beautiful little girl. The girl gazed up at me with sparkling blue eyes. She had straight black hair, a lot like mine, only silkier and finer. She had a bright yellow ribbon in her hair. It matched her short yellow party dress and yellow trainers.

"This is Alicia," the mother announced.

"Hi. I'm Amy," I replied.

"Alicia would like to meet your dummy," the woman said.

"Is he real?" Alicia asked.

I didn't know how to answer that question. "He's a real dummy," I told Alicia.

64

I propped Slappy up in my arms and slipped my hand into his back. "This is Slappy," I told the little girl. "Slappy, this is Alicia."

"How do you do?" I made Slappy say.

Alicia and her mother both laughed. Alicia stared up at the dummy with her sparkling blue eyes.

"How old are you?" I made Slappy say.

Alicia held up three fingers. "I'm fffree," she told him.

"Would you like to shake hands with Slappy?" I asked.

Alicia nodded.

I lowered the dummy a little. I pushed forward Slappy's right hand. "Go ahead," I urged Alicia. "Take his hand."

Alicia reached up and grabbed Slappy's hand. She giggled.

"Happy Birthday," Slappy said.

Alicia shook his hand gently. Then she started to back away.

"We can't wait to see your show," Alicia's mother said to me. "I know the kids are going to love it."

"I hope so!" I replied. My stomach fluttered again. I was still really nervous.

"Let go!" Alicia cried. She tugged at Slappy's hand. She giggled. "He won't let go!"

Alicia's mum laughed. "What a funny dummy!" She grabbed Alicia's other hand. "Let

65

go of the dummy, honey. We have to get every-one in their seats for the show."

Alicia tugged a little harder. "But he won't let go of *me*, Mummy!" she cried. "He wants to shake hands!"

Alicia gave a hard tug. But her tiny hand was still wrapped up inside Slappy's. She giggled. "He likes me. He won't let go."

"Oh, look," her mother said, glancing to the door. "Phoebe and Jennifer just arrived. Let's go and say hi."

Alicia tried to follow her mum, but Slappy held tight to her hand. Alicia's smile faded. "Let *go!*" she insisted.

I saw that several kids had gathered around. They watched Alicia tug at Slappy's hand.

"Let go! Let me go!" Alicia cried angrily.

I leaned over to examine Slappy's hand. To my surprise, it appeared that his hand had clenched tightly around hers.

Alicia gave a hard tug. "Ow! He's hurting me, Mummy!"

More kids came over to watch. Some of them were laughing. Two little dark-haired boys exchanged frightened glances.

"Please—make him let go!" Alicia wailed. She tugged again and again.

I froze in panic. My mind whirred. I tried to think of what to do.

Had Alicia got her hand caught somehow?

Slappy's hand couldn't really close around hers—could it?

Alicia's mother was staring at me angrily. "Please let Alicia's hand out," she said impatiently.

"He's hurting me!" Alicia cried. "Ow! He's squeezing my hand!"

The room grew very quiet. The other kids were all watching now. Their eyes wide. Their expressions confused.

I didn't know what to do. I had no control for Slappy's hands.

My heart pounded in my chest. I tried to make a joke of it. "Slappy really likes you!" I told Alicia.

But the little girl was sobbing now. Little tears rolled down her cheeks. "Mummy—make him stop!"

I pulled my hand out from Slappy's back. I grabbed his wooden hand between my hands. "Let go of her, Slappy!" I demanded.

I tried pulling the fingers open.

But I couldn't budge them.

"What is wrong?" Alicia's mother was screaming. "Is her hand caught? What are you doing to her?"

"He's hurting me!" Alicia wailed. "Owwww! He's squeezing me!"

Several kids were crying now. Mothers rushed across the room to comfort them.

Alicia's sobs rose up over the frightened cries of the other three-year-olds. The harder she tugged, the tighter the wooden hand squeezed.

"Let go, Slappy!" I shrieked, pulling his fingers. "Let go! Let go!"

"I don't understand!" Alicia's mother cried. She began frantically tugging my arm. "What are you doing? Let her go! Let her go!"

"Owwwww!" Alicia uttered a high, heart-breaking wail. "Make him stop! It hurts! It hurts!"

And then Slappy suddenly tilted his head back. His eyes opened wide, and his mouth opened in a long, evil laugh.

I burst into the house and let the screen door slam behind me. I had taken the city bus to Logan Street. Then I had run the six blocks to my house with Slappy hanging over my shoulder.

"Amy, how did it go?" Mum called from the kitchen. "Did you get a lift? I thought we were supposed to come and pick you up."

I didn't answer her. I was sobbing too hard. I ran down the hall to my room and slammed the door.

I hoisted Slappy off my shoulder and threw him into the wardrobe. I never wanted to see him again. Never.

I caught a glimpse of myself in the dresser mirror. My cheeks were swollen and puffy from crying. My eyes were red. My hair was wet and tangled, and matted to my forehead.

I took several deep breaths and tried to stop crying.

I kept hearing that poor little girl's screams in

69

my ears. Slappy finally let go of her after he uttered his ugly laugh.

But Alicia couldn't stop crying. She was so frightened! And her little hand was red and swollen.

The other kids were all screaming and crying, too.

Alicia's mother was furious. She called Margo's dad out from the kitchen. She was shaking and sputtering with anger. She said she was going to sue The Party House.

Margo's dad quietly asked me to leave. He led me to the front door. He said it wasn't my fault. But he said the kids were too frightened of Slappy now. There was no way I could do my show.

I saw Margo hurrying over to me. But I turned and ran out of the door.

I had never been so upset. I didn't know what to do. A light rain had started to come down. I watched rainwater flow down the kerb and into the drain. I wanted to flow away with it.

Now I threw myself on to my bed.

I kept picturing little Alicia, screaming and crying, trying to twist out of Slappy's grasp.

Mum knocked hard on my bedroom door. "Amy? Amy—what are you doing? What's wrong?"

"Go away!" I wailed. "Just go away."

But she opened the door and stepped into the

room. Sara came in behind her, a confused expression on her face.

"Amy—the show didn't go well?" Mum asked softly.

"Go away!" I sobbed. "Please!"

"Amy, you'll do better next time," Sara said, stepping up to the bed. She put a hand on my trembling shoulder.

"Shut up!" I cried. "Shut up, Miss Perfect!"

I didn't mean to sound so angry. I was out of control.

Sara stepped back, hurt.

"Tell us what happened," Mum insisted. "You'll feel better if you tell us."

I pulled myself up until I was sitting on the edge of the bed. I wiped my eyes and brushed my wet hair off my face.

And then, suddenly, the whole story burst out of me.

I told how Slappy had grabbed Alicia's hand and wouldn't let go. And how all the kids were crying. And the parents were all screaming and making a fuss. And how I had to leave without doing my act.

And then I leaped to my feet, threw my arms around my mum, and started to sob again.

She stroked my hair, the way she used to do when I was a little girl. She kept whispering, "Ssshh shhhh shhhh."

Slowly, I began to calm down.

71

"This is so weird," Sara murmured, shaking her head.

"I'm a little worried about you," Mum said, holding my hands. "The little girl got her hand caught. That's all. You don't really believe that the dummy grabbed her hand—do you?"

Mum stared at me hard, studying me.

She thinks I'm crazy, I realized. She thinks I'm totally messed up.

I decided I'd better not insist that my story was true. I shook my head. "Yeah. I guess her hand got caught," I said, lowering my eyes to the floor.

"Maybe you should put Slappy away for a while," Mum suggested, biting her bottom lip.

"Yeah. You're right," I agreed. I pointed. "I already put him in the wardrobe."

"Good idea," Mum replied. "Leave him in there for a while. I think you've been spending too much time with that dummy."

"Yeah. You need a new hobby," Sara chimed in.

"It wasn't a hobby!" I snapped.

"Well, leave him in the wardrobe for a few days—okay, Amy?" Mum said.

I nodded. "I never want to see him again," I muttered.

I thought I heard a sigh from inside the wardrobe. But, of course, that was my imagination.

"Get yourself cleaned up," Mum instructed.

"Wash your face. Then come to the kitchen and I'll make you a snack."

"Okay," I agreed.

Sara followed Mum out the door. "Weird," I heard Sara mutter. "Amy is getting so weird."

Margo called after dinner. She said she felt terrible about what had happened. She said her dad didn't blame me. "He wants to give you another chance," Margo told me. "Maybe with older kids."

"Thanks," I replied. "But I've put Slappy away for a while. I don't know if I want to be a ventriloquist any more."

"At the party today—what happened?" Margo asked. "What went wrong?"

"I don't really know," I said. "I don't really know."

That night, I went to bed early. Before I turned out the light, I glanced at the wardrobe door. It was closed tightly.

Having Slappy shut up in the wardrobe made me feel safer.

I fell asleep quickly. I slept a deep, dreamless sleep.

When I awoke the next morning, I sat up and rubbed my eyes.

Then I heard Sara's angry screams down the hall.

"Mum! Dad! Mum! Hurry!" Sara was shouting. "Come and see what Amy's done now!"

I shut my eyes, listening to my sister's screams.

What now? I thought with a shudder. What now?

"Ohh!" I let out a low cry when I saw that my wardrobe door was open a crack.

My heart pounding, I climbed out of bed and began running down the hall to Sara's room. Mum, Dad and Jed were already on their way.

"Mum! Dad! Look what she did!" Sara screamed.

"Oh, no!" I heard Mum and Dad shriek.

I stopped in the doorway, peered in—and gasped.

Sara's bedroom walls! They were smeared with red paint!

Someone had taken a thick paintbrush and had scrawled AMY AMY AMY AMY in huge red letters all over Sara's walls.

"Noooo!" I moaned. I covered my mouth with both hands to stop the sound.

My eyes darted from wall to wall, reading my name over and over.

AMY AMY AMY AMY.

Why *my* name?

I suddenly felt sick. I swallowed hard, trying to force back my nausea.

I blinked several times, trying to blink the ugly red scrawls away.

AMY AMY AMY AMY.

"Why?" Sara asked me in a trembling voice. She adjusted her nightshirt and leaned against her chest of drawers. "Why, Amy?"

I suddenly realized that everyone was staring at me.

"I—I—I—" I sputtered.

"Amy, this cannot continue," Dad said solemnly. His expression wasn't angry. It was sad.

"We'll get you some help, dear," Mum said. She had tears in her eyes. Her chin trembled.

Jed stood silently with his arms crossed in front of his pyjama top.

"Why, Amy?" Sara demanded again.

"But—I *didn't!*" I finally choked out.

"Amy—no stories," Mum said softly.

"But, Mum—I didn't do it!" I insisted shrilly.

"This is serious," Dad murmured, rubbing his whiskery chin. "Amy, do you realize how serious this is?"

Jed reached out two fingers and rubbed them

over one of the red paint scrawls. "Dry," he reported.

"That means it was done early in the night," Dad said, his eyes locked on me. "Do you realize how bad this is? This isn't just mischief."

I took a deep breath. My whole body was shaking. "Slappy did it!" I blurted out. "I'm not crazy, Dad! I'm not! You've got to believe me! Slappy did it!"

"Amy, please—" Mum said softly.

"Come with me!" I cried. "I'll prove it. I'll prove that Slappy did it. Come on!"

I didn't wait for them to reply. I turned and bolted from the room.

I flew down the hall. They all followed silently behind me.

"Is Amy sick or something?" I heard Jed ask my parents.

I didn't hear the answer.

I burst into my room. They hurried close behind.

I stepped up to the wardrobe and pulled the door open.

"See?" I cried, pointing to Slappy. "See? That proves it! Slappy did it!"

I pointed triumphantly at Slappy. "See? See?"

The dummy sat cross-legged on the wardrobe floor. His head stood erect on his narrow shoulders. He appeared to grin up at us.

Slappy's left hand rested on the wardrobe floor. His right hand was in his lap.

And in his right hand he clutched a fat paintbrush.

The bristles on the brush were caked with red paint.

"I *told* you Slappy did it!" I cried, stepping back so the others could get a better view.

But everyone remained silent. Mum and Dad frowned and shook their heads.

Jed's giggle broke the silence. "This is dumb," he told Sara.

Sara lowered her eyes and didn't reply.

"Oh, Amy," Mum said, sighing. "Did you really think you could blame it on the dummy by putting the paintbrush in his hand?"

"Huh?" I cried. I didn't understand what Mum was saying.

"Did you really expect us to believe this?" Dad asked softly. His eyes stared hard into mine.

"Did you think you could put the brush into Slappy's hand, and make us think he painted your name on Sara's walls?"

"But I *didn't*!" I shrieked.

"When did he learn how to spell?" Jed chimed in.

"Be quiet, Jed," Dad said sharply. "This is serious. It isn't a joke."

"Sara, take Jed out of here," Mum instructed. "The two of you go to the kitchen and get breakfast started."

Sara began to guide Jed to the door. But he pulled away. "I want to stay!" he cried. "I want to see how you punish Amy."

"Get out!" Mum cried, shooing him away with both hands.

Sara tugged him out of the room.

I was shaking all over. I narrowed my eyes at Slappy. Had his grin grown even wider?

I stared at the paintbrush in his hand. The red paint on the bristles blurred, blurred until I saw only red.

I blinked several times and turned back to my parents. "You really don't believe me?" I asked softly, my voice trembling.

They shook their heads. "How can we believe you, dear?" Mum replied.

"We can't believe that a wooden dummy has been doing these horrible things in Sara's room," Dad added. "Why don't you tell us the truth, Amy?"

"But I *am!*" I protested.

How could I prove it to them? How?

I let out an angry cry and slammed the wardrobe door shut.

"Let's try to calm down," Mum urged quietly. "Let's all get dressed and have some breakfast. We can talk about this when we're feeling better."

"Good idea," Dad replied, still squinting at me through his glasses. He was studying me as if he'd never seen me before.

He scratched his bald head. "Guess I'll have to call a painter for Sara's room. It'll take at least two coats to cover up the red."

They turned and made their way slowly from my room, talking about how much it was going to cost to have my sister's room painted.

I stood in the centre of the room and shut my eyes. Every time I closed them, I saw red. All over Sara's wall:

AMY AMY AMY AMY.

"But I didn't do it!" I cried out loud.

My heart pounding, I spun around. I grabbed the knob and jerked open the wardrobe door.

79

I grabbed Slappy by the shoulders of his grey jacket and pulled him up from the floor.

The paintbrush fell from his hand. It landed with a thud beside my bare foot.

I shook the dummy angrily. Shook him so hard that his arms and legs swung back and forth, and his head snapped back.

Then I lifted him so that we were eye to eye.

"Admit it!" I screamed, glaring into his grinning face. "Go ahead! Admit that you did it! Tell me that you did it!"

The glassy blue eyes gazed up at me.

Lifelessly.

Blankly.

Neither of us moved.

And then, to my horror, the wooden lips parted. The red mouth slowly opened.

And Slappy let out a soft, evil, '*Hee hee hee.*"

"I can't come over," I told Margo glumly. I was sprawled on top of my bed, the phone pressed against my ear. "I'm not allowed out of my room all day."

"Huh? Why?" Margo demanded.

I sighed. "If I told you, Margo, you wouldn't believe me."

"Try me," she replied.

I decided not to tell her. I mean, my whole family thought I was crazy. Why should my best friend think it, too?

"Maybe I'll tell you about it when I see you," I said.

Silence at the other end.

Then Margo uttered, "Wow."

"Wow? What does wow mean?" I cried.

"Wow. It must be pretty bad if you can't talk about it, Amy."

"It—it's just weird," I stammered. "Can we change the subject?"

Another silence. "Daddy has a birthday party for six-year-olds coming up, Amy. And he wondered—"

"No. Sorry," I broke in quickly. "I've put Slappy away."

"Excuse me?" Margo reacted with surprise.

"I've put the dummy away," I told her. "I'm finished with that. I'm not going to be a ventriloquist any more."

"But, Amy—" Margo protested. "You *loved* playing with those dummies. And you said you wanted to make some money, remember? So Daddy—"

"No," I repeated firmly. "I changed my mind, Margo. I'm sorry. Tell your dad I'm sorry. I—I'll tell you about it when I see you."

I swallowed hard. And added: "*If* I ever see you."

"You sound terrible," Margo replied softly. "Should I come over to your house? I think I could get my dad to drop me off."

"I'm totally grounded," I said unhappily. "No visitors."

I heard footsteps in the corridor. Probably Mum or Dad checking up on me. I wasn't allowed to be on the phone, either.

"Got to go. Bye, Margo," I whispered. I hung up the phone.

Mum knocked on my bedroom door. I recognized her knock. "Amy, want to talk?" she called in.

"Not really," I replied glumly.

"As soon as you tell the truth, you can come out," Mum said.

"I know," I muttered.

"Why don't you just tell the truth now? It's such a beautiful day," Mum called in. "Don't waste the whole day in your room."

"I—I don't feel like talking now," I told her.

She didn't say anything else. But I could hear her standing out there. Finally I heard her footsteps padding back down the corridor.

I grabbed my pillow and buried my face in it.

I wanted to shut out the world. And think.

Think. Think. Think.

I wasn't going to confess to a crime I didn't do. No way.

I was going to find a way to prove to them that Slappy was the culprit. And I was going to prove to them that I wasn't crazy.

I had to show them that Slappy wasn't an ordinary dummy.

He was alive. And he was evil.

But how could I prove it?

I climbed to my feet and began pacing back and forth. I stopped at the window and gazed out at the front garden.

83

It *was* a beautiful spring day. Bright yellow tulips bobbed in the flower patch in front of my window. The sky was a solid blue. The twin maple trees in the centre of the garden were starting to unfurl fresh leaves.

I took a deep breath. The air smelled so fresh and sweet.

I saw Jed and a couple of his friends. They were Rollerblading down the pavement. Laughing. Having a good time.

And I was a prisoner. A prisoner in my room.

All because of Slappy.

I spun away from the window and stared at the wardrobe door. I had shoved Slappy into the back of the wardrobe and shut the door tightly.

I'm going to catch you in the act, Slappy, I decided.

That's how I'm going to prove I'm not crazy.

I'm going to stay up all night. I'm going to stay up *every* night. And the first time you creep out of the wardrobe, I'll be awake. And I'll follow you.

And I'll make sure that everyone sees what you are doing.

I'll make sure that everyone sees that *you* are the evil one in this house.

I felt so upset. I knew I wasn't really thinking clearly.

But having a plan made me feel a little better.

Taking one last glance at the wardrobe door, I crossed the room to my desk and started to do my homework.

Mum and Dad let me come out for dinner.

Dad had grilled hamburgers in the backyard, the first barbecue of spring. I love grilled hamburgers, especially when they're charred really black. But I could barely taste my food. I guess I felt too excited and nervous about trapping Slappy.

No one talked much.

Mum kept chattering to Dad about the vegetable garden and what she wanted to plant. Sara talked a little about the mural she had started to paint in her room. Jed kept complaining about how he had wrecked his knee Rollerblading.

No one spoke to me. They kept glancing over the table at me. Studying me like I was some kind of zoo animal.

I asked to be excused before dessert.

I usually stay up till ten. But a little after nine, I decided to go to bed.

I was wide awake. Eager to trap Slappy.

I turned out the light and tucked myself in. Then I lay staring up at the shifting shadows on the bedroom ceiling, waiting, waiting . . .

Waiting for Slappy to come creeping out of the wardrobe.

I must have fallen asleep.

I tried not to. But I must have drifted off anyway.

I was startled awake by sounds in the room.

I raised my head, instantly alert. And listened.

The scrape of feet on my carpet. A soft rustling.

A shiver of fear ran down my back. I felt goosebumps up and down my arms.

Another low sound. So near my bed.

I reached forward quickly. Clicked on the bed table lamp.

And cried out.

"Jed—what are you *doing* in here?" I shrieked.

He stood blinking at me in the centre of the room. One leg of his blue pyjama trousers had rolled up. His red hair was matted against one side of his head.

"What are you doing in my room?" I demanded breathlessly.

He squinted at me. "Huh? Why are you yelling at me? You *called* me, Amy."

"I—I *what*?" I sputtered.

"You called me. I heard you." He rubbed his eyes with his fingers and yawned. "I was asleep. You woke me up."

I lowered my feet to the floor and stood up. My legs felt shaky and weak. Jed had really scared me.

"I was asleep, too," I told him. "I didn't call you."

"Yes, you did," he insisted. "You told me to come to your room." He bent to pull

87

down the pyjama leg.

"Jed, you just woke *me* up," I replied. "So how could I call you?"

He scratched his hair. He yawned again. "You mean I dreamed it?"

I studied his face. "Jed—did you sneak into my room to play some kind of prank?" I demanded sternly.

He wrinkled his face up, tried to appear innocent.

"*Did* you?" I demanded. "Were you going into the wardrobe to do something with Slappy?"

"No way!" he protested. He started to back out of the room. "I'm telling the truth, Amy. I thought you called me. That's all."

I squinted hard at him, trying to decide if he was telling the truth. I let my eyes wander around the room. Everything seemed okay. Dennis lay in the armchair, his head in his lap.

The wardrobe door remained closed.

"It was a dream, that's all," Jed repeated. "Good night, Amy."

I said good night. "Sorry I got upset, Jed. It's been a bad day."

I listened to him pad back to his room.

The cat poked his head into my room, his eyes gleaming like gold. "Go to sleep, George," I whispered. "You go to sleep, too, okay?" He obediently turned and disappeared.

I clicked off the bed table lamp and settled back into bed.

Jed was telling the truth, I decided. He seemed as confused as I was.

My eyes suddenly felt heavy. As if there were hundred-pound weights over them. I let out a loud yawn.

I felt so sleepy. And the pillow felt so soft and warm.

But I couldn't let myself fall back to sleep.

I had to stay awake. Had to wait for Slappy to make his move.

Did I drift back to sleep? I'm not sure.

A loud *click* made my eyes shoot open wide.

I raised my head in time to see the wardrobe door start to open.

The room lay in darkness. No light washed in from the window. The door was a black shadow, sliding slowly, slowly.

My heart began to pound. My mouth suddenly felt dry as cotton wool.

The wardrobe door slid slowly, silently.

A low *creak*.

And then a shadow stepped out from behind the dark door.

I squinted hard at it. Not moving a muscle.

Another *creak* of the door.

The figure took another silent step. Out of the wardrobe. Another step. Another. Making its way past my bed, to the bedroom door.

89

Slappy.

Yes!

Even in the night blackness I could see his large, rounded head. I watched his skinny arms dangle at his sides, the wooden hands bobbing as he moved.

The heavy leather shoes slid over my carpet. The thin, boneless legs nearly collapsed with each shuffling step.

Like a scarecrow, I thought, gripped with horror.

He walks like a scarecrow. Because he has no bones. No bones at all.

Up and down, his whole body bobbed as he crept away.

I waited until he slithered and scraped out of the door and into the hall. Then I jumped to my feet.

I took a deep breath and held it.

Then I tiptoed through the darkness after him.

Here we go! I told myself. *Here we go!*

I stopped at the bedroom door and poked my head into the hall. Mum keeps a small night-light on all night just outside her bedroom door. It cast dim yellow light over the other end of the hall.

Peering into the light, I watched Slappy pull himself silently towards Sara's room. The big shoes shuffled along the carpet. Slappy's body bobbed and bent. The big, wooden hands nearly dragged along the floor.

When my chest started to ache, I realized I hadn't taken a breath. As silently as I could, I let out a long whoosh of air. Then I took another deep breath and started to follow Slappy down the hall.

I had a sudden impulse to shout: "Mum! Dad!"

They would burst out of their room and see Slappy standing there in the middle of the hall.

But, no.

I didn't want to shout for them now. I wanted

91

to see where Slappy was heading. I wanted to see what he planned to do.

I took a step. The floorboard creaked under my bare foot.

Did he hear me?

I pressed my back against the wall, tried to squeeze myself flat in the deep shadows.

I peered through the dim yellow light at him. He kept bobbing silently along. His shoulders rode up and down with each shuffling step.

He was just outside Sara's room when he turned around.

My heart stopped.

I ducked low. Dropped back into the bathroom.

Had he seen me?

Had he turned around because he knew I was there?

I shut my eyes. Waited. Listened.

Listened for him to come scraping back. Listened for him to turn around and come back to get me.

Silence.

I swallowed hard. My mouth felt so dry. My legs were trembling. I grabbed the tile wall to steady myself.

Still silent out there.

I gathered up my courage and slowly, slowly poked my head out into the hall.

Empty.

I squinted towards Sara's room in the yellow light.

No one there.

He's in Sara's room, I told myself. He's doing something terrible in Sara's room. Something I'll be blamed for.

Not *this* time, Slappy! I silently vowed.

This time you're going to be caught.

Pressing against the wall, I crept down the hall.

I stopped in Sara's doorway.

The night-light was plugged in across from Sara's room. The light was brighter there.

I squinted into her bedroom. I could see the mural she had started to paint. A beach scene. The ocean. A broad, yellow beach. Kites flying over the beach. Kids building a sand castle in one corner. The mural was tacked up, nearly covering the entire wall.

Where was Slappy?

I took a step into the room—and saw him.

Standing at her paint table.

I saw his big wooden hand fumble over the table of supplies. Then he grabbed a paintbrush in one hand.

He raised and lowered the brush, as if pretending to paint the air.

Then I saw him dip the paintbrush in a jar of paint.

Slappy took a step towards the mural. Then another step.

He stood for a moment, admiring the mural.

He raised the paintbrush high.

That's when I burst into the room.

I dived towards the dummy just as he raised the paintbrush to the mural.

I grabbed the paintbrush with one hand. Wrapped my other hand around his waist. And tugged him back.

The dummy kicked both legs and tried to punch me with his fists.

"Hey!" a startled voice shouted.

The light clicked on.

Slappy went limp on my arm. His head dropped. His arms and legs dangled to the floor.

Sitting up in bed, Sara gaped at me in horror.

I saw her eyes stop at the paintbrush in my hand.

"Amy—what are you *doing*?" she cried.

And, then, without waiting for an answer, Sara began to shout: "Mum! Dad! Hurry! She's in here again!"

Dad came rumbling in first, adjusting his pyjama trousers. "What's going on? What's the problem?"

Mum followed right behind him, blinking and yawning.

"I—I took this from Slappy," I stammered, holding up the paintbrush. "He—he was going to ruin the mural."

They stared at the paintbrush in my hand.

"I heard Slappy sneak out of the wardrobe," I explained breathlessly. "I followed him into Sara's room. I grabbed him just before—before he did something terrible."

I turned to Sara. "You saw Slappy—right? You saw him?"

"Yeah," Sara said, still in bed, her arms crossed over her chest. "I see Slappy. You're carrying him on your arm."

The dummy hung over my arm, its head nearly hitting the floor.

"No!" I cried to Sara. "You saw him sneak into your room—right? That's why you turned on the light?"

Sara rolled her eyes. "I saw *you* come into my room," she replied. "You're *carrying* the dummy, Amy. You're holding the dummy—and the brush."

"But—but—but—" I sputtered.

My eyes darted from face to face. They all stared back at me as if I had just landed on Earth in a flying saucer.

No one in my family was going to believe me. No one.

The next morning, Mum hung up the phone as I came down for breakfast. "You're wearing shorts to school?" she asked, eyeing my outfit— olive-green shorts and a red, sleeveless T-shirt.

"The radio said it's going to be hot," I replied.

Jed and Sara were already at the table. They glanced up from their cereal bowls, but didn't say anything.

I poured myself a glass of grape juice. I'm the only one in my family who doesn't like orange juice. I guess I *am* totally weird.

"Who were you talking to on the phone?" I asked Mum. I took a long drink.

"Uh . . . Dr Palmer's secretary," she replied hesitantly. "You have purple above your lip," she told me, pointing.

I wiped the grape juice off with a napkin. "Dr Palmer? Isn't she a shrink?" I asked.

Mum nodded. "I tried to get an appointment for today. But she can't see you until Wednesday."

"But, Mum—!" I protested.

Mum placed a finger over her mouth. "Sssshhh. No discussion."

"But, Mum—!" I repeated.

"Ssshhh. Just talk to her once, Amy. You might enjoy it. You might think it's helpful."

"Yeah. Sure," I muttered.

I turned to Sara and Jed. They stared down at their cereal bowls.

I sighed and set the juice glass down in the sink.

I knew what this meant. It meant that I had until Wednesday to prove to my family that I wasn't a total wack job.

In the canteen at school, Margo begged me to tell her what was going on with me. "Why were you locked up in your room all day yesterday?" she demanded. "Come on, Amy—spill."

"It's no big deal," I lied.

No way I was going to tell her.

I didn't need the story going around school that Amy Kramer believes her ventriloquist's dummy is alive.

I didn't need everyone whispering about me

and staring at me the way everyone in my family did.

"Dad wants to know if you'll change your mind about the birthday party," Margo said. "If you want to perform with Slappy, you can—"

"No. Forget it!" I interrupted. "I put Slappy in the wardrobe, and he's staying there. For ever."

Margo's eyes went wide. "Okay. Okay. Wow. You don't have to bite my head off."

"Sorry," I said quickly. "I'm a little stressed out these days. Here. Want this?" I handed her the brownie Mum had packed.

"Thanks," Margo replied, surprised.

"Later," I said. I crinkled up my lunch bag, tossed it in the bin, and hurried away.

In my room that night, I couldn't concentrate on my homework. I kept staring at the calendar.

Monday night. I had only two nights to prove that I wasn't crazy, that Slappy really was doing these horrible things.

I slammed my history book shut. No way I could read about the firing on Fort Sumter tonight.

I paced back and forth for a while. Thinking. Thinking hard. But getting nowhere.

What could I do?

What?

After a while, my head felt about to split open. I reached up both hands and tugged at my hair.

98

"Aaaaagh!" I let out a furious cry. Of anger. Of frustration.

Maybe I'll just get rid of Slappy, I decided. Maybe I'll take him outside and throw him in the bin.

And that will end the whole problem.

The idea made me feel a little better.

I turned and took two steps towards the wardrobe.

But I stopped with a gasp when I saw the doorknob slowly turn.

As I stared in shock, the wardrobe door swung open.

Slappy stepped out.

He slumped forward and stopped a few feet in front of me.

His blue eyes glared up at me. His grin grew wider.

"Amy," he rasped, "it's time you and I had a little talk."

"Amy, now you are my slave," Slappy said. His threat came out in a harsh, cold rasp. The eerie voice made me shiver.

I stared back at him. I couldn't reply.

I gaped into those glassy blue eyes, that red-lipped smirk.

"You read the ancient words that bring me to life," the dummy whispered. "And now you will serve me. You will do everything I ask."

"No!" I finally managed to choke out. "No! Please—!"

"Yes!" he cried. The grinning wooden head bobbed up and down, nodding. "Yes, Amy! You are my slave now! My slave for ever."

"I w-won't!" I stammered. "You can't make me—" My voice caught in my throat. My legs wobbled like rubber. My knees buckled, and I nearly fell.

Slappy raised one hand and grabbed my wrist. I felt the cold, wooden fingers tighten around me. "You will do as I tell you—from now on," the dummy whispered. "Or else . . ."

"Let go of me!" I cried. I struggled to tug my arm free. But his grasp was too tight. "Or else *what*?" I cried.

"Or else I will destroy your sister's mural," Slappy replied. His painted grin grew wider. The cold eyes glared into mine.

"Big deal," I muttered. "Do you really think I'll be your slave because you wreck her painting? You've already wrecked Sara's room— haven't you? That doesn't mean I'll be your slave!"

"I'll keep on destroying things," Slappy replied, tightening his grip on my wrist, tugging me down towards him. "Maybe I'll start wrecking your brother's things, too. And you will be blamed, Amy. You will be blamed for it all."

"Stop—" I cried, trying to twist free.

"Your parents are already worried about you—aren't they, Amy?" the dummy rasped in that harsh, cold whispery voice. "Your parents already think you're crazy!"

"Stop! Please—!" I pleaded.

"What do you think they'll do when you start wrecking everything in the house?" Slappy demanded. "What do you think they'll do to you, Amy?"

"Listen to me!" I shrieked. "You can't—"

He jerked my arm hard. "They'll send you

101

away!" he rasped, his eyes flashing wildly. "That's what your parents will do. They'll send you away. And you'll never see them again—except on visiting days!"

He tilted back his wooden head and uttered a shrill laugh.

A low moan escaped my throat. My entire body shuddered with terror.

Slappy tugged me closer. "You will be an excellent slave," he whispered in my ear. "You and I will have many good years together. You will devote your life to me."

"No!" I cried. "No, I won't!"

I sucked in a deep breath. Then I swung my arm hard, as hard as I could.

I caught the dummy by surprise.

Before he could let go of my wrist, I pulled him off balance.

He let out a startled grunt as I lifted him off the floor.

He's just a dummy, I told myself. *Just a dummy. I can handle him. I can beat him.*

His hand fell off my wrist.

I ducked low. Grabbed his boneless arm with both hands. Swung my shoulder. Flipped him over my back.

He landed hard on his stomach. His head made a loud *clonk* as it hit the floor.

Breathing hard, my heart thudding wildly, I dived.

102

I can handle him. I can beat him.

I tried to pin him to the floor with my knees.

But he spun away and scrambled up, faster than I could believe.

I cried out as he swung his wooden fist.

I tried to dodge away. But he was too fast.

The heavy fist hit me square in the forehead.

My face felt as if it had exploded. Pain shot down my body.

Everything went bright red.

And, holding both sides of my head, I crumpled to the floor.

I can handle him. I can beat him.

The words repeated in my mind.

I blinked my eyes. Raised my head.

I refused to give up.

Through the haze of red, I reached up with both hands.

I grabbed Slappy by the waist and pulled him down.

Ignoring my throbbing forehead, I wrestled him to the ground. He kicked both feet and thrashed his arms wildly. He swung at me, trying to land another blow.

But I dug my knee into his middle. Then I wrapped my hands around his thrashing arms and pinned them to the floor.

"Let go, slave!" he squealed. "I command you—let go!" He struggled and squirmed.

But I held tight.

His eyes darted frantically from side to side.

His wooden jaw clicked open and shut, open

104

and shut, as he strained to squirm free.

"I command you to let go, slave! You have no choice! You must obey me!"

I ignored his shrill cries and swung his arms behind his back. Holding them tightly in place I climbed to my feet.

He tried to kick me with both shoes. But I let go of the arms and grabbed his legs.

I swung him upside down. Once again, his head hit the floor with a *clonk*.

It didn't seem to hurt him a bit.

"Let go! Let go, slave! You will pay! You will pay dearly for this!" He screamed and protested, squirming and swinging his arms.

Breathing hard, I dragged him across the rug—and swung him into the open wardrobe.

He dived quickly, trying to escape.

But I slammed the door in his face. And turned the lock.

With a sigh, I leaned my back against the wardrobe door and struggled to catch my breath.

"Let me out! You can't keep me in here!" Slappy raged.

He began pounding on the door. Then he kicked the door.

"I'll break it down! I really will!" he threatened. He pounded even harder. The big wooden hands thudded against the wooden door.

I turned and saw the door start to give.

He's going to break it open! I realized.

What can I do? What can I do now? I tried to fight back my panic, struggled to think clearly.

Slappy furiously kicked at the door.

I need help, I decided.

I bolted into the hall. Mum and Dad had their bedroom door closed, I saw. Should I wake them up?

No. They wouldn't believe me.

I'd drag them into my room. Slappy would be slumped lifelessly on the wardrobe floor. Mum and Dad would be even more upset about me.

Sara, I thought. Maybe I can convince Sara. Maybe Sara will listen to me.

Her door was open. I burst into her bedroom.

She stood at the mural, brush in hand, dabbing yellow paint on the beach.

She turned as I ran in, and her face tightened in anger. "Amy—what do *you* want?" she demanded.

"You—you've got to believe me!" I sputtered. "I need your help! It wasn't me who did those horrible things. It really wasn't, Sara. It was Slappy. Please—believe me! It was Slappy!"

"Yes. I know," Sara replied calmly.

106

21

"Huh?" My mouth dropped open. I stared at her in surprise. "What did you say?"

Sara set down the paintbrush. She wiped her hands on her grey smock. "Amy—I know it's Slappy," she repeated in a whisper.

"I—I—" I was so stunned, I couldn't speak. "But, Sara—you—"

"I'm sorry. I'm so sorry!" she cried with emotion. She rushed forward and threw her arms around me. She hugged me tightly.

I still didn't believe what she had said. My head was spinning.

I gently pushed her away. "You knew all this time? You knew it was Slappy and not me?"

Sara nodded. "The other night, I woke up. I heard someone in my room. I pretended to be asleep. But I had my eyes open partway."

"And—?" I demanded.

"I saw Slappy," Sara confessed, lowering her eyes. "I saw him carrying a red paintbrush. I saw him painting AMY AMY AMY AMY all over my walls."

"But you didn't tell Mum and Dad?" I cried. "You made them think it was me? And the whole time, you knew the truth?"

Sara kept her eyes on the floor. Her black hair fell over her face. She brushed it back with a quick, nervous sweep of one hand.

"I—I didn't want to believe it," she confessed. "I didn't want to believe that a dummy could walk on its own, that it could be . . . alive."

I glared at her. "And, so—?"

"So I accused you," Sara said with a sob. "I guess the truth was just too scary. I was too frightened, Amy. I *wanted* to believe it was you doing those horrible things. I wanted to pretend it wasn't the dummy."

"You *wanted* to get me in trouble," I accused. "That's why you did it, Sara. That's why you lied to Mum and Dad. You *wanted* to get me in trouble."

She finally raised her face to me. I saw two tears trailing down her cheeks. "Yeah, I guess," she murmured.

She wiped the tears off with her hands. Her green eyes locked on mine. "I—I guess I'm a little jealous of you," she said.

"Huh?" My sister had stunned me again. I squinted at her, trying to make sense of her words. "You?" I cried. "You're jealous of *me*?"

She nodded. "Yeah. I guess. Everything is easy for you. You're so relaxed. Everyone likes your sense of humour. It's not like that for me," Sara explained. "I have to paint to impress people."

I opened my mouth, but no sound came out.

This had to be the biggest surprise of all. Sara jealous of *me*?

Didn't she know how jealous I was of *her*?

I suddenly had a funny feeling in my chest. My eyes brimmed with tears. Strong emotion swept over me like an ocean wave.

I rushed forward and hugged Sara.

For some reason, we both started laughing. I can't explain it. We stood there in the middle of her room, laughing like lunatics.

I guess we were just so glad that the truth was out.

Then Slappy's painted face flashed back into my mind. And I remembered with a chill why I had burst into my sister's room.

"You have to help me," I told her. "Right now."

Sara's smile vanished. "Help you do what?" she demanded.

"We have to get rid of Slappy," I told her. "We have to get rid of him for good."

I tugged her hand. She followed me down the hall.

"But—how?" she asked.

109

Stepping into my room, we both cried out at once.

We heard a final kick—and the wardrobe door swung open.

Slappy burst out, his eyes wild with rage.

"Guess what, slaves?" he rasped. "Slappy wins!"

"Grab him!" I cried to my sister.

I reached out both arms and made a frantic dive for the dummy. But he scampered to the side and slipped away from my tackle.

His blue eyes flashed excitedly. His red lips twisted in an ugly grin.

"Give up, slaves!" he rasped. "You cannot win!"

Sara held back, hands against the door frame. I could see the fear in her eyes.

I made another grab for Slappy. Missed again.

"Sara—help me!" I pleaded.

Sara took a step into the room.

I leaped at Slappy, grabbed one boneless ankle.

With a grunt, he pulled out of my grasp. He darted towards the door—and ran right into Sara.

The collision stunned them both.

Sara staggered back.

Slappy teetered off balance.

I threw myself at him, caught his arms, and pulled them behind his back.

He squirmed and twisted. He kicked out furiously.

But Sara grabbed both of his big leather shoes. "Tie him in a knot!" she cried breathlessly.

He kicked and thrashed.

But we held tight.

I twisted his arms behind him. Twisted them around each other. Twisted. Twisted. Then tied them in as tight a knot as I could.

Slappy squirmed and bucked, grunting loudly, his wooden jaws clicking.

When I glanced up from my work on the arms, I saw that Sara had wrapped his legs in a knot, too.

Slappy tilted back his head and uttered a roar of rage. His eyes slid up into his head so that only the whites showed. "*Put me down, slaves! Put me down at once!*"

With one hand, I grabbed a wad of tissues from my bedside table and jammed it into Slappy's mouth.

He uttered a grunt of protest, then went silent.

"Now what?" Sara cried breathlessly. "Where should we put him?"

My eyes shot around the room. No, I decided. I don't want him in my room. I don't want him in the house.

"Outside," I instructed my sister, holding on to the knotted arms with both of my hands. "Let's get him outside."

Struggling to hold on to the bucking legs, Sara glanced at the clock. "It's after eleven. What if Mum and Dad hear us?"

"I don't care!" I cried. "Hurry! I want him out of here! I never want to see him again!"

We dragged Slappy out into the hall. Mum and Dad's door remained closed.

Good, I thought. They hadn't heard our struggle.

Sara carried him by the knotted legs. I held on to the arms.

Slappy had stopped struggling and squirming. I think he was waiting to see what we were going to do with him. The wad of tissues had silenced his cries.

I didn't know where to take him. I only knew I wanted him out of the house.

We carried him through the darkened living room and out the front door. We stepped into a hot, sticky night, more like summer than spring. A pale sliver of a moon hovered low in a blue-black sky.

There was no breeze. No sounds of any kind. Nothing moved.

Sara and I carried the dummy to the driveway. "Should we take him somewhere on our bikes?" she suggested.

"How will we balance him?" I asked. "Besides, it's too dark. Too dangerous. Let's just carry him a few blocks and dump him somewhere."

"You mean in a dustbin or something?" Sara asked.

I nodded. "That's where he belongs. In the bin."

Luckily, the dummy didn't weigh much at all. We made our way to the road, then carried him to the end of the block.

Slappy remained limp, his eyes rolled up in his head.

At the corner, I spotted two circles of white light approaching. Car headlights. "Quick—!" I whispered to Sara.

We slipped behind a hedge just in time. The car rolled by without slowing.

We waited for the glow of red taillights to disappear in the darkness. Then we continued down the next block, carrying the dummy between us.

"Hey—how about those?" Sara asked, pointing with her free hand.

I squinted to see what she had spotted. A row of metal dustbins lined up at the kerb in front of a dark house across the street.

"Looks good," I said. "Let's shove him in and clamp down the lid. Maybe the dustbin men will haul him away tomorrow."

I led the way across the street—and then

114

stopped. "Sara—wait," I whispered. "I have a better idea."

I dragged the dummy towards the corner. I motioned to the metal drain down at the kerb.

"The sewer?" Sara whispered.

I nodded. "It's perfect." Through the narrow opening at the kerb, I could hear running water far down below. "Come on. Shove him in."

Slappy still didn't move or protest in any way.

I lowered his head to the drain opening. Then Sara and I pushed him in headfirst.

I heard a *splash* and a hard *thud* as he hit the sewer floor.

We both listened. Silence. Then the soft trickle of water.

Sara and I grinned at each other.

We hurried home. I was so happy, I skipped most of the way.

The next morning, Sara and I came to the kitchen for breakfast together. Mum turned from the counter, where she was pouring herself a cup of coffee.

Jed was already at the table, eating his Frosted Flakes. "What's *he* doing down here?" Jed asked.

He pointed across the table.

At Slappy. Sitting in the chair.

Sara and I both gasped.

"Yes. Why is that dummy down here?" Mum asked me. "I found him sitting there when I came in this morning. And why is he so dirty? Where has he been, Amy?"

I could barely choke out a word. "I . . . uh . . . I guess he fell or something," I finally mumbled.

"Well, take him back upstairs," Mum ordered. "He's supposed to be kept in the wardrobe—remember?"

"Uh . . . yeah. I remember," I said, sighing.

"You'll have to clean him up later," Mum said, stirring her coffee. "He looks as if he's been wallowing in the mud."

"Okay," I replied weakly.

I hoisted Slappy up and slung him over my shoulder. Then I started to my room.

"I—I'll come with you," Sara stammered.

"What for?" Mum demanded. "Sit down, Sara,

and eat your breakfast. You're both going to be late."

Sara obediently sat down across from Jed. I made my way down the hall.

I was halfway to my room when Slappy raised his head and whispered in my ear, "Good morning, slave. Did you sleep well?"

I threw him into the wardrobe and locked the door. I could hear him laughing inside. The evil laugh made me shake all over.

What am I going to do now? I asked myself. *What can I do to get rid of this creature?*

The day dragged by. I don't think I heard a word my teacher said.

I couldn't get Slappy's evil, grinning face out of my mind. His raspy voice rattled in my ears.

I won't be your slave! I silently vowed. *I'll get you out of my house—out of my life—if it's the last thing I do!*

That night, I lay wide awake in my bed. How could I sleep, knowing that evil dummy sat in the wardrobe a few feet away?

The night was hot and steamy. I had pushed the window open all the way, but there was no breeze. A fly buzzed by my head, the first fly of spring.

Staring up at the twisting shadows on the ceiling, I brushed the fly away with one hand. As soon as the buzzing vanished, another sound took its place.

A click. A low squeak.

The sound of the wardrobe door opening.

I raised myself up off the pillow. Squinting into the darkness, I saw Slappy creep out of the wardrobe.

He took a few shuffling steps, his big shoes sliding silently over my carpet. He turned.

Was he coming towards my bed?

No.

His head and shoulders bobbed as he pulled himself to the door. Then out into the hall.

He's going to Sara's room, I knew.

But what was he going to do there? Did he plan to pay us back for what we did to him last night?

What new horror was he going to create?

I lowered my feet to the floor, climbed out of bed, and followed him out into the hall.

My eyes adjusted quickly to the dim yellow light from the night-light at the other end of the hall. I watched Slappy slither towards my sister's room. He moved as silently as a shadow.

I held my breath and kept my back against the wall as I followed behind him. When he turned into Sara's room, I stepped away from the wall and started to run.

I reached the bedroom doorway in time to see Slappy pick up a wide paintbrush from Sara's supply table. He took a step towards the mural on the wall.

One step.

And then another small figure leaped out of the darkness.

The lights flashed on.

"Dennis!" I cried.

"*Stand back!*" Dennis ordered in a high, shrill voice. He lowered his wooden head and charged at Slappy.

Sara sat up in her bed and uttered a frightened cry.

I could see the stunned expression on Slappy's face.

Dennis flew at Slappy. He slammed his head into Slappy's middle.

Slappy let out a loud "*Oooof!*" He staggered back. Fell.

A loud *thud* rang through the room as the back of Slappy's head hit Sara's iron bedpost.

I raised both hands to my cheeks and gasped as Slappy's head cracked open.

The wooden head split down the middle.

I watched the evil face crack apart. The wide, shocked eyes slid in different directions. The red lips cracked and fell away.

The head dropped to the floor in two pieces. And then the body collapsed in a heap beside them.

My hands still pressed against my face, my heart pounding, I took a few steps into the room.

Dennis ran past me, out to the hall.

But my eyes were locked on the two pieces of Slappy's head. I stared in horror as an enormous white worm crawled out of one of the pieces. The fat worm slithered and curled to the wall—and vanished into a crack in the skirting board.

Sara climbed out of bed, breathing hard, her face bright red from the excitement.

The wardrobe door swung open. Mum and Dad came bursting out.

"Girls—are you okay?" Dad cried.

We nodded.

"We saw the whole thing!" Mum exclaimed. She threw her arms around me. "Amy, I'm so sorry. I'm so sorry. We should have believed you. I'm so sorry we didn't believe you."

"We believe you now!" Dad declared, staring down at Slappy's broken head, his crumpled body. "We saw everything!"

It was all planned. Sara and I had worked it out before dinner.

Sara convinced Mum and Dad to hide in the wardrobe. Mum and Dad were really creeped out by the way I was acting. They were willing to do anything.

So Sara pretended to go to sleep. Mum and Dad hid in the wardrobe.

I left the wardrobe door unlocked to make it easier for Slappy to get out.

I knew Slappy would creep into Sara's room. I knew Mum and Dad would finally see that I'm not crazy.

And then Jed burst out dressed as Dennis, with Dennis's head propped up on top of his turtleneck sweater.

We knew that would shock Slappy. We knew it would give us a chance to grab him.

We didn't know what a great job Jed would do.

We didn't know that Jed would actually destroy the evil dummy. We didn't know that Slappy's head would crack apart. That was just good luck.

'Hey—where *is* Jed?" I asked, my eyes searching the room.

"Jed? Jed?" Mum called. "Where are you? You did a great job!"

No reply.

No sign of my brother.

"Weird," Sara muttered, shaking her head.

We all trooped down the hall into Jed's room.

We found him in bed, sound asleep. He groggily raised his head from the pillow and squinted at us. "What time is it?" he asked sleepily.

"It's nearly eleven," Dad replied.

"Oh, no!" Jed cried, sitting up. "I'm sorry I forgot to wake up! I forgot I was supposed to dress up like Dennis!"

I felt a shiver run down my back. I turned to my parents. "Then who fought Slappy?" I asked. "Who fought Slappy?"

Say Cheese and Die!

"There's nothing to do in Pitts Landing," Michael Warner said, his hands shoved into the pockets of his faded denim cut-offs.

"Yeah. Pitts Landing is the pits," Greg Banks said.

Doug Arthur and Shari Walker muttered their agreement.

Pitts Landing is the Pits. That was the town slogan, according to Greg and his three friends. Actually, Pitts Landing wasn't very different from a lot of small towns with quiet streets of shady lawns and comfortable, old houses.

But here it was, a balmy autumn afternoon, and the four friends were hanging round Greg's drive, kicking at the gravel, wondering what to do for fun and excitement.

"Let's go to Grover's and see if the new comics have come in," Doug suggested.

"We haven't got any money, Bird," Greg told him.

Everyone called Doug "Bird" because he looked a lot like a bird. A better nickname might have been "Stork". He had long, skinny legs and took long, stork-like steps. Under his thick tuft of brown hair, which he seldom brushed, he had small, bird-like brown eyes and a long nose that curved like a beak. Doug didn't really like being called Bird, but he was used to it.

"We can still *look* at the comics," Bird insisted.

"Until Grover starts shouting at you," Shari said. She puffed out her cheeks and did a pretty good imitation of the gruff store owner: "*Are you paying or staying?*"

"He thinks he's cool," Greg said, laughing at her imitation. "He's such a jerk."

"I think the new *X-Force* is coming in this week," Bird said.

"You should join the X-Force," Greg said, giving his pal a playful shove. "You could be Bird Man. You'd be great!"

"We should *all* join the X-Force," Michael said. "If we were super-heroes, maybe we'd have something to do."

"No, we wouldn't," Shari quickly replied. "There's no crime to fight in Pitts Landing."

"We could fight crabgrass," Bird suggested. He was the joker in the group.

The others laughed. The four of them had been friends for a long time. Greg and Shari lived next door to each other, and their parents were best friends. Bird and Michael lived round the corner.

"How about a baseball game?" Michael suggested. "We could go down to the playground."

"No way," Shari said. "You can't play with only four people." She pushed back a strand of her crimped, black hair that had fallen over her face. Shari was wearing an oversized yellow sweatshirt over bright green leggings.

"Maybe we'll find some other kids there," Michael said, picking up a handful of gravel from the drive and letting it sift through his chubby fingers. Michael had short red hair, blue eyes, and a face full of freckles. He wasn't exactly fat, but no one could ever call him skinny.

"Come on, let's play baseball," Bird urged. "I need the practice. My Little League starts in a couple of days."

"Little League? In the autumn?" Shari asked.

"It's a new autumn league. The first game is on Tuesday after school," Bird explained.

"Hey—we'll come and watch you," Greg said.

"We'll come and watch you strike out," Shari added. She loved teasing Bird.

"What position are you playing?" Greg asked.

"Backstop," Michael cracked.

No one laughed. Michael's jokes always fell flat.

Bird shrugged. "Probably fielding. How

come *you're* not playing, Greg?"

With his big shoulders and muscular arms and legs, Greg was the natural athlete of the group. He was blond and good-looking, with flashing grey-green eyes and a wide, friendly smile.

"My brother Terry was supposed to go and sign me up, but he forgot," Greg said, making a disgusted face.

"Where *is* Terry?" Shari asked. She had a tiny crush on Greg's older brother.

"He's got a job on Saturdays and after school. At the Dairy Freeze," Greg told her.

"Let's go to the Dairy Freeze!" Michael exclaimed enthusiastically.

"We haven't got any money—remember?" Bird said glumly.

"Terry'll give us free cones," Michael said, turning a hopeful gaze on Greg.

"Yeah. Free cones. But no ice cream in them," Greg told him. "You know what a square my brother is."

"This is boring," Shari complained, watching a robin hop across the pavement. "It's boring standing around talking about how bored we are."

"We could *sit down* and talk about how bored we are," Bird suggested, twisting his mouth into the goofy half-smile, he always wore when he was making a stupid joke.

128

"Let's go for a walk or a jog or something," Shari insisted. She made her way across the lawn and began walking, balancing her white high-tops on the edge of the kerb, waving her arms like a tightrope walker.

The boys followed, imitating her in an impromptu game of Follow the Leader, all of them balancing on the kerb edge as they walked.

A curious cocker spaniel came bursting out of the neighbours' hedge, yapping excitedly. Shari stopped to pet him. The dog, its stub of a tail wagging furiously, licked her hand a few times. Then the dog lost interest and disappeared back into the hedge.

The four friends continued down the road, playfully trying to knock each other off the kerb as they walked. They crossed the street and continued on past the school. A couple of boys were shooting baskets, and some little kids playing football on the practice baseball pitch, but no one they knew.

The road curved away from the school. They followed it past familiar houses. Then, just beyond a small wooded area, they stopped and looked up a sloping lawn, the grass uncut for weeks, tall weeds poking out everywhere, the shrubs ragged and overgrown.

At the top of the lawn, nearly hidden in the shadows of enormous, old oak trees, sprawled a large, ramshackle house. The house, anyone could see, had once been grand. It was grey shingle, three stories tall, with a wraparound screened porch, a sloping red roof, and tall chimneys on either end. But the broken windows on the first floor, the cracked, weather-stained shingles, the bare spots on the roof, and the shutters hanging loosely beside the dust-smeared windows were evidence of the house's neglect.

Everyone in Pitts Landing knew it as the Coffman house. Coffman was the name painted on the postbox that tilted on its broken pole over the front path.

But the house had been deserted for years—ever since Greg and his friends could remember.

And people liked to tell weird stories about the house: ghost stories and wild tales about murders and ghastly things that happened there. Most likely, none of them were true.

"Hey—I know what we can do for excitement," Michael said, staring up at the house bathed in shadows.

"Huh? What are you talking about?" Greg asked warily.

"Let's go into the Coffman house," Michael said, starting to make his way across the weed-choked lawn.

"Whoa. Are you crazy?" Greg called, hurrying to catch up with him.

"Let's go in," Michael said, his blue eyes

catching the light of the late afternoon sun filtering down through the tall oak trees. "We wanted an adventure. Something a little exciting, right? Come on—let's check it out."

Greg hesitated and stared up at the house. A cold chill ran down his back.

Before he could reply, a dark form leapt up from the shadows of the tall weeds and attacked him!

Greg toppled backwards onto the ground. "Aah!" he screamed. Then he realized the others were laughing.

"It's that stupid cocker spaniel!" Shari cried. "He followed us!"

"Go home, dog. Go home!" Bird shooed the dog away.

The dog trotted to the kerb, turned round, and stared back at them, its stubby tail wagging furiously.

Feeling embarrassed that he'd become so frightened, Greg slowly pulled himself to his feet, expecting his friends to give him grief. But they were staring up at the Coffman house thoughtfully.

"Yeah, Michael's right," Bird said, slapping Michael hard on the back, so hard Michael winced and turned to push Bird. "Let's see what it's like in there."

"No way," Greg said, hanging back. "I mean,

the place is pretty creepy, don't you think?"

"So?" Shari challenged him, joining Michael and Bird, who repeated her question: "So?"

"So . . . I don't know," Greg replied. He didn't like being the sensible one of the group. Everyone always made fun of the sensible one. He'd rather be the wild and wacky one. But, somehow, he always ended up sensible.

"I don't think we should go in there," he said, staring up at the neglected old house.

"Are you chicken?" Bird asked.

"Chicken!" Michael joined in.

Bird began to cluck loudly, tucking his hands into his armpits and flapping his arms. With his beady eyes and beaky nose, he looked just like a chicken.

Greg didn't want to laugh, but he couldn't help it.

Bird *always* made him laugh.

The clucking and flapping seemed to end the discussion. They were standing at the foot of the broken concrete steps that led up to the screened porch.

"Look. The window next to the front door is broken," Shari said. "We can just reach in and open the door."

"This is cool," Michael said enthusiastically.

"Are we really doing this?" Greg, being the sensible one, had to ask. "I mean—what about Spidey?"

133

Spidey was a weird-looking man of about fifty or sixty they'd all seen lurking about town. He dressed entirely in black and crept along on long, slender legs. He looked just like a black spider, so the kids all called him Spidey.

Most likely he was a homeless person. No one really knew anything about him—where he'd come from, where he lived. But a lot of kids had seen him hanging round the Coffman house.

"Maybe Spidey doesn't like visitors," Greg warned.

But Shari was already reaching in through the broken windowpane to unlock the front door. And after little effort, she turned the brass knob and the heavy wooden door swung open.

One by one, they walked through the front entrance, Greg reluctantly bringing up the rear. It was dark inside the house. Only narrow beams of sunlight managed to trickle down through the heavy trees in front, creating pale circles of light on the worn brown carpet at their feet.

The floorboards squeaked as Greg and his friends made their way past the living room, which was bare except for a couple of overturned grocery shop boxes against one wall.

Spidey's furniture? Greg wondered.

The living room carpet, as threadbare as the one by the front door, had a dark oval stain in the centre of it. Greg and Bird, stopping in the

134

doorway, both noticed it at the same time.

"Think it's blood?" Bird asked, his tiny eyes lighting up with excitement.

Greg felt a chill on the back of his neck. "Probably ketchup," he replied. Bird laughed and slapped him hard on the back.

Shari and Michael were exploring the kitchen. They were staring at the dust-covered kitchen worktop as Greg came up behind them. He saw immediately what had captured their attention. Two fat, grey mice were standing on the worktop, staring back at them.

"They're cute," Shari said. "They look just like cartoon mice."

The sound of her voice made the two rodents scamper along the worktop, round the sink, and out of sight.

"They're gross," Michael said, making a disgusted face. "I think they were rats—not mice."

"Rats have long tails. Mice don't," Greg told him.

"They were definitely rats," Bird muttered, pushing past them and out into the hall. He disappeared towards the front of the house.

Shari reached up and pulled open a cupboard unit over the worktop. Empty. "I suppose Spidey never uses the kitchen," she said.

"Well, I didn't *think* he was a gourmet chef," Greg joked.

He followed her into the long, narrow dining

135

room, as bare and dusty as the other rooms. A low chandelier still hung from the ceiling, so brown with caked dust, it was impossible to tell that it was glass.

"Looks like a haunted house," Greg said softly.

"Boo," Shari replied.

"There's not much to see in here," Greg complained, following her back to the dark hallway. "Unless you get a thrill from cobwebs."

Suddenly, a loud *crack* made him jump.

Shari laughed and squeezed his shoulder.

"What was *that*?" he cried, unable to stifle his fear.

"Old houses *do* things like that," she said. "They make noises for no reason at all."

"I think we should leave," Greg insisted, embarrassed again that he'd acted so frightened. "I mean, it's boring in here."

"It's sort of exciting being somewhere we're not supposed to be," Shari said, peering into a dark, empty room—probably a study or something at one time.

"I suppose so," Greg replied uncertainly.

They bumped into Michael. "Where's Bird?" Greg asked.

"I think he went down to the basement," Michael replied.

"Huh? The basement?"

Michael pointed to an open door at the right,

off the hall. "The stairs are there."

The three of them made their way to the top of the stairs. They peered down into the darkness. "Bird?"

From somewhere deep in the basement, his voice floated up to them in a horrified scream: "Help! It's got me! Somebody—please help! It's *got* me!"

"It's got me! It's got me!"

At the sound of Bird's terrified cries, Greg pushed past Shari and Michael, who stood frozen in open-mouthed horror. Practically flying down the steep staircase, Greg called out to his friend, "I'm coming, Bird! What *is it*?"

His heart pounding, Greg stopped at the bottom of the stairs, every muscle tight with fear. His eyes searched frantically through the smoky light pouring in from the basement windows up near the ceiling.

"Bird?"

There he was, sitting comfortably, calmly, on an overturned metal dustbin, his legs crossed, a broad smile on his birdlike face. "Gotcha," he said softly, and burst out laughing.

"What *is* it? What *happened*?" came the frightened voices of Shari and Michael. They clamoured down the stairs, coming to a stop beside Greg.

It took them only a few seconds to realize the situation.

"Another stupid joke?" Michael asked, his voice still trembling with fear.

"Bird—you were winding us up again?" Shari sighed, shaking her head.

Enjoying his moment, Bird nodded, with his peculiar half-grin. "You lot are too easy," he scoffed.

"But, Doug—" Shari started. She only called him Doug when she was upset with him. "Haven't you ever heard of the boy who cried wolf? What if something really bad happens one day, and you really need help, and we think you're just kidding?"

"What could happen?" Bird replied smugly. He stood up and gestured around the basement. "Look—it's brighter down here than upstairs."

He was right. Sunlight from the back garden cascaded down through four long windows at ground level, near the ceiling of the basement.

"I still think we should get out of here," Greg insisted, his eyes moving quickly round the large, cluttered room.

Behind Bird's overturned dustbin stood a makeshift table made out of a sheet of plywood resting on four paint cans. A nearly flat mattress, dirty and stained, rested against the wall, a faded wool blanket folded at the foot.

"Spidey must *live* down here!" Michael exclaimed.

Bird kicked his way through a pile of empty food boxes that had been tossed all over the floor—TV dinners, mostly. "Hey, a Hungry Man dinner!' he exclaimed. "Where does Spidey heat these up?"

"Maybe he eats them frozen," Shari suggested. "You know. Like ice pops."

She made her way towards a towering oak wardrobe and pulled open the doors. "Wow! This is *excellent*!" she declared. "Look!" She pulled out a ratty-looking fur coat and wrapped it round her shoulders. "Excellent!" she repeated, twirling in the old coat.

From across the room, Greg could see that the wardrobe was stuffed with old clothing. Michael and Bird hurried to join Shari and began pulling out strange-looking pairs of bell-bottom trousers, yellowed dress shirts with pleats down the front, tie-dyed neckties that were about a foot wide, and brightly-coloured scarves and bandannas.

"Hey, you lot—" Greg warned. "Don't you think maybe those belong to somebody?"

Bird spun round, a fuzzy red boa wrapped around his neck and shoulders. "Yeah. These are Spidey's dressing-up clothes," he cracked.

"How about this *baad* hat?" Shari said, turning round to show off the bright purple, wide-brimmed hat she had pulled on.

140

"Great," Michael said, examining a long blue cape. "This stuff must be at least twenty-five years old. It's awesome. How could someone just leave it here?"

"Maybe they're coming back for it," Greg suggested.

As his friends explored the contents of the wardrobe, Greg wandered to the other end of the basement. A large boiler occupied the far wall, its ducts covered in thick cobwebs. Partially hidden by the boiler ducts, Greg could see stairs, probably leading to an outside exit.

Wooden shelves lined the adjoining wall, cluttered with old paint cans, rags, newspapers, and rusty tools.

Whoever lived here must have been a real handyman, Greg thought, examining a wooden worktable in front of the shelves. A metal vice was clamped to the edge of the worktable. Greg turned the handle, expecting the jaws of the vice to open.

But to his surprise, as he turned the vice handle, a door just above the worktable popped open. Greg pulled the door all the way open, revealing a hidden cabinet shelf.

Resting on the shelf was a camera.

For a long moment, Greg just stared at the camera.

Something told him the camera was hidden away for a reason.

Something told him he shouldn't touch it. He should close the secret door and walk away.

But he couldn't resist it.

He reached onto the hidden shelf and took the camera in his hands.

It pulled out easily. Then, to Greg's surprise, the door instantly snapped shut with a loud *bang*.

Weird, he thought, turning the camera in his hands.

What a strange place to leave a camera. Why would someone put it here? If it were valuable enough to hide in a secret cabinet, why didn't they take it with them?

Greg eagerly examined the camera. It was large and surprisingly heavy, with a long lens.

Perhaps a telephoto lens, he thought.

Greg was very interested in cameras. He had a cheap automatic camera, which took okay photos. But he was saving his pocket money in the hopes of buying a really good camera with a lot of lenses.

He loved looking at camera magazines, studying the different models, picking out the ones he wanted to buy.

Sometimes he daydreamed about travelling around the world, going to amazing places, mountaintops and hidden jungle rivers. He'd take photos of everything he saw and become a famous photographer.

His camera at home was just too crummy. That's why all his pictures came out too dark or too light, and everyone in them had glowing red dots in their eyes.

Greg wondered if this camera was any good.

Raising the viewfinder to his eye, he sighted around the room. He came to a stop on Michael, who was wearing two bright yellow feather boas and a white Stetson hat and had climbed to the top of the steps to pose.

"Wait! Hold it!" Greg cried, moving closer, raising the camera to his eye. "Let me take your picture, Michael."

"Where'd you find that?" Bird asked.

"Does that thing have film in it?" Michael demanded.

"I don't know," Greg said. "Let's see."

Leaning against the railing, Michael struck what he considered a sophisticated pose.

Greg pointed the camera up and focused carefully. It took a short while for his finger to locate the shutter button. "Okay, ready? Say cheese."

"Cheddar," Michael said, grinning down at Greg as he held his pose against the railing.

"Very funny. Michael's a riot," Bird said sarcastically.

Greg centred Michael in the viewfinder frame, then pressed the shutter button.

The camera clicked and flashed.

Then it made an electronic whirring sound. A slot pulled open on the bottom, and a cardboard square slid out.

"Hey—it's one of those automatic-developing cameras," Greg exclaimed. He pulled the square of cardboard out and examined it. "Look—the picture is starting to develop."

"Let me see," Michael called down, leaning on the railing.

But before he could start down the stairs, everyone heard a loud crunching sound.

They all looked up to the source of the sound— and saw the banister break away and Michael go sailing over the edge.

"Noooooo!" Michael screamed as he toppled to the floor, arms outstretched, the feather boas flying behind him like animal tails.

He turned in the air, then hit the concrete hard on his back, his eyes frozen wide in astonishment and fright.

He bounced once.

Then cried out again: "My ankle! Owwww! My ankle!" He grabbed at the injured ankle, then quickly let go with a loud gasp. It hurt too much to touch it.

"*Ohhh*—my ankle!"

Still holding the camera and the photo, Greg rushed to Michael. Shari and Bird did the same.

"We'll go and get help," Shari told Michael, who was still on his back, groaning in pain.

But then they heard the ceiling creak.

Footsteps. Above them.

Someone was in the house.

Someone was approaching the basement stairs.

They were going to be caught.

The footsteps above grew louder.

The four friends exchanged frightened glances. "We've got to get *out* of here," Shari whispered.

The ceiling creaked.

"You can't leave me here!" Michael protested. He pulled himself into a sitting position.

"Quick—stand up," Bird instructed.

Michael struggled to his feet. "I can't stand on this foot." His face revealed his panic.

"We'll help you," Shari said, turning her eyes to Bird. "I'll take one arm. You take the other."

Bird obediently moved forward and pulled Michael's arm around his shoulder.

"Okay, let's move!" Shari whispered, supporting Michael from the other side.

"But how do we get out?" Bird asked breathlessly.

The footsteps grew louder. The ceiling creaked under their weight.

"We can't go up the stairs," Michael whispered, leaning on Shari and Bird.

"There's another staircase behind the boiler," Greg told them, pointing.

"It leads out?" Michael asked, wincing from his ankle pain.

"Probably."

Greg led the way. "Just pray the door isn't padlocked or something."

"We're praying. We're praying!" Bird declared.

"We're outta here!" Shari said, groaning under the weight of Michael's arm.

Leaning heavily against Shari and Bird, Michael hobbled after Greg, and they made their way to the stairs behind the boiler. The stairs, they saw, led to wooden double doors up on ground level.

"I don't see a padlock," Greg said warily. "Please, doors—be open!"

"*Hey—who's down there?*" an angry man's voice called from behind them.

"It's—it's Spidey!" Michael stammered.

"Hurry!" Shari urged, giving Greg a frightened push. "Come *on!*"

Greg put the camera down on the top step. Then he reached up and grabbed the handles of the double doors.

"*Who's down there?*"

Spidey sounded closer, angrier.

"The doors could be locked from the outside," Greg whispered, hesitating.

"Just *push* them, man!" Bird pleaded.

Greg took a deep breath and pushed with all his strength.

The doors didn't budge.

"We're trapped," he told them.

"Now what?" Michael whined.

"Try again," Bird urged Greg. "Maybe they're just stuck." He slid out from under Michael's arm. "Here. I'll help you."

Greg moved over to give Bird room to come up beside him. "Ready?" he asked. "One, two, three—*push*!"

Both boys pushed against the heavy wooden doors with all their might.

And the doors swung open.

"Okay! *Now* we're outta here!" Shari declared happily.

Picking up the camera, Greg led the way out. The back garden, he saw, was as weed-choked and overgrown as the front. An enormous limb had fallen off an old oak tree, probably during a storm, and was lying half in the tree, half on the ground.

Somehow, Bird and Shari managed to drag Michael up the steps and onto the grass. "Can

149

you walk? Try it," Bird said.

Still leaning against the two of them, Michael reluctantly pushed his foot down on the ground. He lifted it. Then pushed it again. "Hey, it feels a bit better," he said, surprised.

"Then let's go," Bird said.

They ran to the overgrown hedge that edged along the side of the garden, Michael on his own now, stepping gingerly on the bad ankle, doing his best to keep up. Then, staying in the shadow of the hedge, they made their way round the house to the front.

"All *right!*" Bird cried happily as they reached the street. "We made it!"

Gasping for breath, Greg stopped at the kerb and turned back towards the house. "Look!" he cried, pointing up to the living room window.

A dark figure stood in the window, hands pressed against the glass.

"It's Spidey," Shari said.

"He's just—staring at us," Michael cried.

"Weird," Greg said. "Let's go."

They didn't stop till they got to Michael's house, a sprawling ranch-style house behind a shady front lawn.

"How's the ankle?" Greg asked.

"It's loosened up a lot. It doesn't even hurt that much," Michael said.

"Man, you could've been *killed!*" Bird declared,

wiping sweat off his forehead with the sleeve of his T-shirt.

"Thanks for reminding me," Michael said drily.

"Lucky thing you've got all that extra padding," Bird teased.

"Shut up," Michael muttered.

"Well, you boys wanted adventure," Shari said, leaning back against the trunk of a tree.

"That bloke Spidey is definitely weird," Bird said, shaking his head.

"Did you see the way he was staring at us?" Michael asked. "All dressed in black and everything? He looked like some kind of zombie or something."

"He saw us," Greg said softly, suddenly feeling a chill of dread. "He saw us very clearly. We'd better stay away from there."

"What for?" Michael demanded. "It isn't his house. He's just sleeping there. We could get the police on him."

"But if he's really loony or something, there's no telling what he might do," Greg replied thoughtfully.

"Aw, he's not going to do anything," Shari said quietly. "Spidey doesn't want trouble. He just wants to be left alone."

"Yeah," Michael agreed quickly. "He didn't want us messing around with his stuff. That's why he shouted like that and came after us."

151

Michael was leaning over, rubbing his ankle. "Hey, where's my picture?" he demanded, straightening up and turning to Greg.

"Huh?"

"You know. The picture you took. With the camera."

"Oh. Right." Greg suddenly realized he still had the camera gripped tightly in his hand. He put it down carefully on the grass and reached into his back pocket. "I put it here when we started to run," he explained.

"Well? Did it come out?" Michael demanded.

The three of them huddled round Greg to get a view of the photo.

"Whoa—hold on a minute!" Greg cried, staring hard at the small, square photo. "Something's wrong. What's going *on* here?"

The four friends gaped at the photograph in Greg's hand, their mouths dropping open in surprise.

The camera had caught Michael in midair as he fell through the broken railing to the floor.

"That's impossible!" Shari cried.

"You took the picture *before* I fell!" Michael declared, grabbing the photo out of Greg's hand so that he could study it close up. "I remember it."

"You remembered wrong," Bird said, moving to get another look at it over Michael's shoulder. "You were falling, man. What a great action shot." He picked up the camera. "This is a good camera you stole, Greg."

"I didn't steal it"—Greg started—"I mean, I didn't realize—"

"I *wasn't* falling!" Michael insisted, tilting the picture in his hand, studying it from every angle. "I was posing, remember? I had a big, goofy smile on my face, and I was posing."

"I remember the goofy smile," Bird said, handing the camera back to Greg. "Do you have any *other* expression?"

"You're not funny, Bird," Michael muttered. He pocketed the picture.

"Weird," Greg said. He glanced at his watch. "Hey—I've got to get going."

He said goodbye to the others and headed for home. The afternoon sun was lowering behind a cluster of palm trees, casting long, shifting shadows over the pavement.

He had promised his mother he'd straighten up his room and help with the vacuuming before dinner. And now he was late.

What was that strange car in the drive? he wondered, jogging across the neighbour's lawn towards his house.

It was a navy-blue Taurus estate car. Brand new.

Dad's picked up our new car! he realized.

Wow! Greg stopped to admire it. It still had the sticker glued to the door window. He pulled open the driver's door, leaned in, and smelled the vinyl upholstery.

Mmmmmmm. That new-car smell.

He inhaled deeply again. It smelled so good. So fresh and new.

He closed the door hard, appreciating the solid *clunk* it made as it closed.

154

What a great new car, he thought excitedly.

He raised the camera to his eye and took a few steps back off the drive.

I've *got* to take a picture of this, he thought. To remember what the car was like when it was totally new.

He backed up until he had framed the entire profile of the car in the viewfinder. Then he pressed the shutter button.

As before, the camera clicked loudly, the flash flashed, and with an electronic *whirr*, a square undeveloped photo of grey and yellow slid out of the bottom.

Carrying the camera and the snapshot, Greg ran into the house through the front door. "I'm home!" he called. "Down in a minute!" And hurried up the carpeted stairs to his room.

"Greg? Is that you? Your father's home," his mother called from downstairs.

"I know. Be right down. Sorry I'm late!" Greg shouted back.

I'd better hide the camera, he decided. If Mum or Dad see it, they'll want to know whose it is and where I got it. And I won't be able to answer those questions.

"Greg—did you see the new car? Are you coming down?" his mother called impatiently from the bottom of the stairs.

"I'm coming!" he yelled.

His eyes searched frantically for a good hiding place.

Under his bed?

No. His mum might vacuum under there and discover it.

Then Greg remembered the secret compartment in his headboard. He had discovered the compartment years ago when his parents had bought him a new bedroom set. Quickly, he shoved the camera in.

Peering into the mirror above his chest of drawers, he gave his blond hair a quick brush, rubbed a black soot smudge off his cheek with one hand, then started for the door.

He stopped at the doorway.

The snapshot of the car. Where had he put it?

It took a few seconds to remember that he had tossed it onto his bed. Curious about how it had come out, he turned back to retrieve it.

"Oh, no!"

He uttered a low cry as he gazed at the photograph.

What's going on here? Greg wondered.

He brought the photo up close to his face.

This isn't right, he thought. How can this *be*?

The blue Taurus estate car in the photo was a mess. It looked as if it had been in a terrible accident. The windscreen was shattered. Metal was twisted and bent. The door on the driver's side had caved in.

The car appeared *wrecked*!

"This is impossible!" Greg uttered aloud.

"Greg, where *are* you?" his mother called. "We're all hungry, and you're keeping us waiting."

"Sorry," he answered, unable to take his eyes off the photo. "Coming."

He shoved it into the top drawer of his chest of drawers and made his way downstairs. The image of the wrecked car burned in his mind.

Just to make sure, he crossed the living room and peeped out of the front window at the drive.

157

There stood the new car, sparkling in the glow of the setting sun. Shiny and perfect.

He turned and walked into the dining room where his brother and his parents were already sitting. "The new car is awesome, Dad," Greg said, trying to shake the photo's image from his thoughts.

But he kept seeing the twisted metal, the caved-in driver's door, the shattered windscreen.

"After dinner," Greg's dad announced happily, "I'm taking you all for a drive in the new car!"

"Mmmm. This is great chicken, Mum," Greg's brother Terry said, chewing as he talked.

"Thanks for the compliment," Mrs Banks said drily, "but it's veal—not chicken."

Greg and his dad burst out laughing. Terry's face grew bright red. "Well," he said, still chewing, "it's such excellent veal, it tastes as good as chicken!"

"I don't know why I bother to cook," Mrs Banks sighed.

Mr Banks changed the subject. "How are things at the Dairy Freeze?" he asked.

"We ran out of vanilla this afternoon," Terry said, forking a small potato and shoving it whole into his mouth. He chewed it briefly, then gulped it down. "People were annoyed about that."

"I don't think I can go for the car ride," Greg said, staring down at his dinner, which he'd hardly touched. "I mean—"

"Why not?" his father asked.

"Well . . ." Greg searched his mind for a good reason. He needed to make one up, but his mind was a blank.

He couldn't tell them the truth.

That he had taken a photograph of Michael, and it showed Michael falling. Then a few seconds later, Michael had fallen.

And now he had taken one of the new car. And the car was wrecked in the photo.

Greg didn't really know what it meant. But he was suddenly filled with this powerful feeling, of dread, of fear, of . . . he didn't know what.

A kind of troubled feeling he'd never had before.

But he couldn't tell them any of that. It was too weird. Too *crazy.*

"I . . . made plans to go over to Michael's," he lied, staring down at his plate.

"Well, phone him and tell him you'll see him tomorrow," Mr Banks said, slicing his veal. "That's no problem."

"Well, I'm kind of not feeling very well, either," Greg said.

"What's wrong?" Mrs Banks asked with instant concern. "Have you got a temperature? I thought you looked a little flushed when you came in."

"No," Greg replied uncomfortably. "No temperature. I just feel tired, not very hungry."

"Can I have your chicken—I mean, veal?" Terry asked eagerly. He reached for his fork across the table and nabbed the cutlet off Greg's plate.

"Well, a nice drive might make you feel better," Greg's dad said, eyeing Greg suspiciously. "You know, some fresh air. You can stretch out in the back if you want."

"But, Dad—" Greg stopped. He had used up all the excuses he could think of. They would *never* believe him if he said he needed to stay at home and do homework on a Saturday night!

"You're coming with us, and that's final," Mr Banks said, still studying Greg closely. "You've been dying for this new car to arrive. I really don't understand your problem."

Neither do I, Greg admitted to himself.

I don't understand it at all. Why am I so afraid of going in the new car? Just because there's something wrong with that stupid camera?

I'm being silly, Greg thought, trying to shake away the feeling of dread that had taken away his appetite.

"Okay, Dad. Great," he said, forcing a smile. "I'll come."

"Are there any more potatoes?" Terry asked.

"It's so easy to drive," Mr Banks said, as he accelerated onto the street. "It handles like a small car, not like an estate car."

"Plenty of room back here, Dad," Terry said, scooting low in the back seat beside Greg, raising his knees to the back of the front seat.

"Hey, look—there's a drinks holder that pulls out from the dashboard!" Greg's mother exclaimed. "That's handy."

"Awesome, Mum," Terry said sarcastically.

"Well, we've never had a drinks holder before," Mrs Banks replied. She turned back to the two boys. "Are your seat belts buckled? Do they work properly?"

"Yeah. They're okay," Terry replied.

"They checked them at the showroom, before I took the car," Mr Banks said, signalling to move into the left lane.

A truck roared by, spitting a cloud of exhaust behind it. Greg stared out of the front window.

His door window was still covered by the new car sticker.

Mr Banks pulled off the road, onto a nearly empty four-lane motorway that curved towards the west. The setting sun was a red ball low on the horizon in a charcoal-grey sky.

"Put the pedal to the metal, Dad," Terry urged, sitting up and leaning forward. "Let's see what this car can do."

Mr Banks obediently pressed his foot on the accelerator. "The cruising speed seems to be about sixty," he said.

"Slow down," Mrs Banks scolded. "You know the speed limit is fifty-five."

"I'm just testing it," Greg's dad said defensively. "You know. Making sure the transmission doesn't slip or anything."

Greg stared at the glowing speedometer. They were doing seventy now.

"Slow down. I mean it," Mrs Banks insisted. "You're acting like a crazy teenager."

"That's me!" Mr Banks replied, laughing. "This is *awesome*!" he said, imitating Terry, ignoring his wife's pleas to slow down.

They roared past a couple of small cars in the right lane. Headlights of cars moving towards them were a bright white blur in the darkening night.

"Hey, Greg, you've been awfully quiet," his mother said. "You feeling okay?"

163

"Yeah. I'm okay," Greg said softly.

He wished his dad would slow down. He was doing seventy-five now.

"What do you think, Greg?" Mr Banks asked, steering with his left hand as his right hand searched the dashboard. "Where's the light switch? I should turn on my headlights."

"The car's great," Greg replied, trying to sound enthusiastic. But he couldn't shake away the fear, couldn't get the photo of the mangled car out of his mind.

"Where's that stupid light switch? It's got to be here somewhere," Mr Banks said.

As he glanced down at the unfamiliar dashboard, the car swerved to the left.

"Dad—look out for that truck!" Greg screamed.

Horns blared.

A powerful blast of air swept over the estate car, like a giant ocean wave pushing it to the side.

Mr Banks swerved the estate car to the right. The truck rumbled past.

"Sorry," Greg's dad said, eyes straight ahead, slowing the car to sixty, fifty-five, fifty . . .

"I *told* you to slow down," Mrs Banks scolded, shaking her head. "We could've been killed!"

"I was trying to find the lights," he explained. "Oh. Here they are. On the steering wheel." He clicked on the headlights.

"You boys okay?" Mrs Banks asked, turning to check on them.

"Yeah. Fine," Terry said, sounding a little shaken. The truck would have hit his side of the car.

"I'm okay," Greg said. "Can we go back now?"

"Don't you want to keep going?" Mr Banks asked, unable to hide his disappointment. "I thought we'd keep going to Santa Clara. Stop and get some ice cream or something."

"Greg's right," Mrs Banks said softly to her husband. "Enough for tonight, dear. Let's turn round."

"The truck didn't come *that* close," Mr Banks argued. But he obediently turned off the motorway and they headed for home.

Later, safe and sound up in his room, Greg took the photograph out of the drawer and examined it. There was the new car, the driver's side caved in, the windscreen shattered.

"Weird," he said aloud, and placed the photo in the secret compartment in his headboard where he had stashed the camera. "Definitely weird."

He pulled the camera out of its hiding place and turned it around in his hands.

I'll try it once more, he decided.

He walked to his chest of drawers and aimed at the mirror above it.

I'll take a picture of myself in the mirror, he thought.

He raised the camera, then changed his mind. That won't work, he realized. The flash will reflect back and spoil the photo.

Gripping the camera in one hand, he made his way across the landing to Terry's room. His brother was at his desk, typing away on his computer keyboard, his face bathed in the blue light of the monitor screen.

"Terry, can I take your photo?" Greg asked meekly, holding up the camera.

Terry typed some more, then looked up from the screen. "Hey—where'd you get the camera?"

"Uh . . . Shari lent it to me," Greg told him, thinking quickly. Greg didn't like lying. But he didn't feel like explaining to Terry how he and his friends had sneaked into the Coffman house and he had made off with the camera.

"So can I take your picture?" Greg asked.

"I'll probably break your camera," Terry joked.

"I think it's already broken," Greg told him. "That's why I want to test it on you."

"Go ahead," Terry said. He stuck out his tongue and crossed his eyes.

Greg snapped the shutter. An undeveloped photo slid out of the slot in front.

"Thanks. See you." Greg headed for the door.

"Hey—don't I get to see it?" Terry called after him.

"If it comes out," Greg said, and hurried across the landing to his room.

He sat down on the edge of the bed. Holding the photo in his lap, he stared at it intently as it developed. The yellows filled in first. Then the reds appeared, followed by shades of blue.

"Whoa," Greg muttered as his brother's face came into view. "There's something definitely wrong here."

In the photo, Terry's eyes weren't crossed, and his tongue wasn't sticking out. His expression was grim, frightened. He looked very upset.

As the background came into focus, Greg had another surprise. Terry wasn't in his room. He was outdoors. There were trees in the background. And a house.

Greg stared at the house. It looked so familiar.

Was that the house across the street from the playground?

He took one more look at Terry's frightened expression. Then he tucked the photo and the camera into his secret headboard compartment and carefully closed it.

The camera must be broken, he decided, getting changed for bed.

It was the best explanation he could come up with.

Lying in bed, staring up at the shifting shadows on the ceiling, he decided not to think about it any more.

A broken camera wasn't worth worrying about.

On Tuesday afternoon after school, Greg hurried to meet Shari at the playground to watch Bird's Little League game.

It was a warm autumn afternoon, the sun high in a cloudless sky. The outfield grass had been freshly mowed and filled the air with its sharp, sweet smell.

Greg crossed the grass and squinted into the bright sunlight, searching for Shari. Both teams were warming up on the sides of the pitch, yelling and laughing, the sound of balls popping into gloves competing with their loud voices.

A few parents and several kids had come to watch. Some were standing around, some sitting in the low bleachers along the first base line.

Greg spotted Shari behind the backstop and waved to her. "Did you bring the camera?" she asked eagerly, running over to greet him.

He held it up.

"Excellent," she exclaimed, grinning. She reached for it.

"I think it's broken," Greg said, holding on to the camera. "The photos just don't come out right. It's hard to explain."

"Maybe it's not the photos. Maybe it's the photographer," Shari teased.

"Maybe I'll take a photo of you getting a knuckle sandwich," Greg threatened. He raised the camera to his eye and pointed it at her.

"Snap that, and I'll take a picture of you *eating* the camera," Shari threatened playfully. She reached up quickly and pulled the camera from his hand.

"What do you want it for, anyway?" Greg asked, making a half-hearted attempt to grab it back.

Shari held it away from his outstretched hand. "I want to take Bird's picture when he comes to bat. He looks just like an ostrich at the plate."

"I heard that." Bird appeared beside them, pretending to be insulted.

He looked ridiculous in his starched white uniform. The shirt was too big, and the trousers were too short. The cap was the only thing that fitted. It was blue, with a silver dolphin over the peak and the words: PITTS LANDING DOLPHINS.

"What kind of name is 'Dolphins' for a baseball team?" Greg asked, grabbing the peak and turning the cap backwards on Bird's head.

"All the other caps were taken," Bird answered. "We had a choice between the Zephyrs and the Dolphins. None of us knew what Zephyrs were, so we picked Dolphins."

Shari eyed him up and down. "Maybe you lot should play in your ordinary clothes."

"Thanks for the encouragement," Bird replied. He spotted the camera and took it from her. "Hey, you've brought the camera. Has it got any film in it?"

"Yeah. I think so," Greg told him. "Let me see." He reached for the camera, but Bird swung it out of his grasp.

170

"Hey—are you going to share this thing, Greg?" he asked.

"Huh? What do you mean?" Greg reached again for the camera, and again Bird swung it away from him.

"I mean, we all risked our lives down in that basement getting it, right?" Bird said. "We should all share it."

"Well . . ." Greg hadn't thought about it. "I suppose you're right, Bird. But I'm the one who found it. So—"

Shari grabbed the camera out of Bird's hand. "I told Greg to bring it so we could take your photo when you're batting."

"As an example of good form?" Bird asked.

"As a *bad* example," Shari said.

"You lot are just jealous," Bird replied, frowning, "because I'm a natural athlete, and you can't cross the road without falling on your faces." He turned the cap back round to face the front.

"Hey, Bird—get back here!" one of the coaches called from the playing field.

"I've got to go," Bird said, giving them a quick wave and starting to trot back to his teammates.

"No. Wait. Let me take a fast picture now," Greg said.

Bird stopped, turned round, and struck a pose.

"No. I'll take it," Shari insisted.

She started to raise the camera to her eye,

pointing it towards Bird. And as she raised it, Greg grabbed for it.

"Let *me* take it!"

And the camera went off. Clicked and then flashed.

An undeveloped photo slid out.

"Hey, why'd you do that?" Shari asked angrily.

"Sorry," Greg said. "I didn't mean to—"

She pulled the photo out and held it in her hand. Greg and Bird came close to watch it develop.

"What the heck is *that*?" Bird cried, staring hard at the small square as the colours brightened and took shape.

"Oh, wow!" Greg cried.

The photo showed Bird sprawled unconscious on his back on the ground, his mouth twisted open, his neck bent at a frightening angle, his eyes shut tight.

"Hey—what's wrong with this stupid camera?" Bird asked, grabbing the photo out of Shari's hand. He tilted it from side to side, squinting at it. "It's out of focus or something."

"Weird," Greg said, shaking his head.

"*Hey, Bird—get over here!*" the Dolphins' coach called.

"Coming!" Bird handed the picture back to Shari and jogged over to his teammates.

Whistles blew. The two teams stopped their practising and trotted to the benches along the third base line.

"How did this *happen*?" Shari asked Greg, shielding her eyes from the sun with one hand, holding the photo close to her face with the other. "It really looks like Bird is lying on the ground, knocked out or something. But he was standing right in front of us."

"I don't get it. I really don't," Greg replied thoughtfully. "The camera keeps doing that."

Carrying the camera at his side, swinging it by its slender strap, he followed her to a shady spot beside the benches.

"Look how his neck is bent," Shari continued. "It's so *awful*."

"There's definitely something wrong with the camera," Greg said. He started to tell her about the photo he'd taken of the new car, and the picture of his brother Terry. But she interrupted before he could get the words out.

"—And that picture of Michael. It showed him falling down the stairs before he even fell. It's just so strange."

"I know," Greg agreed.

"Let me see that thing," Shari said and pulled the camera from his hand. "Is there any film left?"

"I can't tell," Greg admitted. "I couldn't find a film roll or anything."

Shari examined the camera closely, rolling it over in her hands. "It doesn't say anywhere. How can you tell if it's loaded or not?"

Greg shrugged.

The baseball game got under way. The Dolphins were the visiting team. The other team, the Cardinals, jogged out to take their positions on the field.

A kid in the benches dropped his lemonade can. It hit the ground and spilled, and the kid started to cry. An old estate car filled with teenagers cruised by, its radio blaring, its horn honking.

"Where do you put the film in?" Shari asked impatiently.

Greg stepped closer to help her examine it. "Here, I think," he said, pointing. "Doesn't the back come off?"

Shari fiddled with it. "No, I don't think so. Most of these automatic-developing cameras load in the front."

She pulled at the back, but the camera wouldn't open. She tried pulling off the bottom. No better luck. Turning the camera, she tried pulling off the lens. It wouldn't budge.

Greg took the camera from her. "There's no slot or opening in the front."

"Well, what kind of camera is it anyway?" Shari demanded.

"Uh . . . let's see." Greg studied the front, examined the top of the lens, then turned the camera over and studied the back.

He stared up at her with a surprised look on his face. "There's no brand name. Nothing."

"How can a camera not have a name?" Shari shouted in exasperation. She snatched the camera away from him and examined it closely, squinting her eyes against the bright afternoon sunshine.

Finally, she handed the camera back to him, defeated. "You're right, Greg. No name. No words of any kind. Nothing. What a stupid camera," she added angrily.

"Whoa. Hold on," Greg told her. "It's not my camera, remember? I didn't buy it. I took it from the Coffman house."

"Well, let's at least work out how to open it up and look inside," Shari said.

The first Dolphin batter popped up to the second baseman. The second batter struck out on three straight swings. The dozen or so spectators shouted encouragement to their team.

The little kid who had dropped his drink continued to cry. Three kids cycled by on bikes, waving to friends on the teams, but not stopping to watch.

"I've tried and tried, but I can't work out how to open it," Greg admitted.

"Give it to me," Shari said and grabbed the camera away from him. "There has to be a button or something. There has to be some way of opening it. This is ridiculous."

When she couldn't find a button or lever of any kind, she tried pulling the back off once again, prising it with her fingernails. Then she tried turning the lens, but it wouldn't turn.

"I'm not giving up," she said, gritting her teeth. "I'm not. This camera has to open. It *has* to!"

"Give up. You're going to wreck it," Greg warned, reaching for it.

"Wreck it? How could I wreck it?" Shari demanded. "It has no moving parts. Nothing!"

"This is impossible," Greg said.

Making a disgusted face, she handed the camera to him. "Okay, I give up. Look it over yourself, Greg."

He took the camera, started to raise it to his face, then stopped.

Uttering a low cry of surprise, his mouth dropped open and his eyes gaped straight ahead. Startled, Shari turned to follow his shocked gaze.

"Oh *no!*"

There on the ground a few metres outside the first base line, lay Bird. He was sprawled on his back, his neck bent at an odd and unnatural angle, his eyes shut tight.

"Bird!" Shari cried.

Greg's breath caught in his throat. He felt as if he were choking. "Oh!" he finally managed to cry out in a shrill, raspy voice.

Bird didn't move.

Shari and Greg, running side by side at full speed, reached him together.

"Bird?" Shari knelt down beside him. "Bird?"

Bird opened one eye. "Gotcha," he said quietly. The weird half-smile formed on his face, and he exploded into high-pitched laughter.

It took Shari and Greg a while to react. They both stood open-mouthed, gaping at their laughing friend.

Then, his heart beginning to slow to normal, Greg reached down, grabbed Bird with both hands, and pulled him roughly to his feet.

"I'll hold him while you hit him," Greg offered, holding Bird from behind.

"Hey, wait—" Bird protested, struggling to

squirm out of Greg's grasp.

"Good plan," Shari said, grinning.

"Ow! Hey—let go! Come on! Let go!" Bird protested, trying unsuccessfully to wrestle free. "Come on! What's your problem? It was a joke, okay?"

"Very funny," Shari said, giving Bird a playful punch on the shoulder. "You're hilarious, Bird."

Bird finally freed himself with a hard tug and danced away from both of them. "I just wanted to show you how pathetic it is to get all worked up about that stupid camera."

"But, Bird—" Greg started.

"It's just broken, that's all," Bird said, brushing blades of recently cut grass off his uniform trousers. "You think because it showed Michael falling down those stairs, there's something strange about it. But that's stupid. Really stupid."

"I *know*," Greg replied sharply. "But how do you explain it?"

"I told you, man. It's wrecked. Broken. That's it."

"*Bird—get over here!*" a voice called, and Bird's fielder's glove came flying at his head. He caught it, waved with a grin to Shari and Greg, and jogged to the outfield along with the other members of the Dolphins.

Carrying the camera tightly in one hand, Greg

179

led the way to the benches. He and Shari sat down on the end of the bottom bench.

Some of the spectators had lost interest in the game already and had left. A few kids had taken a baseball off the field and were having their own game of catch behind the benches. Across the playground, four or five kids were getting a game of football started.

"Bird is such a dork," Greg said, his eyes on the game.

"He scared me to death," Shari exclaimed. "I really thought he was hurt."

"What a clown," Greg muttered.

They watched the game in silence for a while. It wasn't terribly interesting. The Dolphins were losing 12–3 going into the third inning. None of the players were very good.

Greg laughed as a Cardinal batter, a kid from their class named Joe Garden, slugged a ball that sailed out to the field and right over Bird's head.

"That's the third ball that's gone over his head!" Greg cried.

"I suppose he lost it in the sun!" Shari exclaimed, joining in the laughter.

They both watched Bird's long legs storking after the ball. By the time he managed to catch up with it and heave it towards the diamond, Joe Garden had already rounded the bases and scored.

There were loud *boos* from the benches.

The next Cardinal batter stepped up to the plate. A few more kids climbed down from the benches, having seen enough.

"It's so hot here in the sun," Shari said, shielding her eyes with one hand. "And I've got lots of homework. Want to leave?"

"I just want to see the next inning," Greg said, watching the batter swing and miss. "Bird is coming up next inning. I want to stay and *boo* him."

"What are friends for?" Shari said sarcastically.

It took a long while for the Dolphins to get the third out. The Cardinals batted around their entire order.

Greg's T-shirt was drenched with sweat by the time Bird came to the plate in the top of the fourth.

Despite the loud *booing* from Shari and Greg, Bird managed to punch the ball past the shortstop for a single.

"Lucky hit!" Greg yelled, cupping his hands into a megaphone.

Bird pretended not to hear him. He tossed away his batter's helmet, adjusted his cap, and took a short lead off first base.

The next batter swung at the first pitch and fouled it off.

"Let's go," Shari urged, pulling Greg's arm.

"It's too hot. I'm dying of thirst."

"Let's just see if Bird—"

Greg didn't finish his sentence.

The batter hit the next ball hard. It made a loud *thunk* as it left the bat.

A dozen people—players and spectators—cried out as the ball flew across the pitch, a sharp line drive, and slammed into the side of Bird's head with another *thunk*.

Greg watched in horror as the ball bounced off Bird and dribbled away onto the grass. Bird's eyes went wide with disbelief, confusion.

He stood frozen in place on the base path for a long moment.

Then both of his hands shot up above his head, and he uttered a shrill cry, long and loud, like the high-pitched whinny of a horse.

His eyes rolled up in his head. He sank to his knees. Uttered another cry, softer this time. Then collapsed, sprawling onto his back, his neck at an unnatural angle, his eyes closed.

He didn't move.

In seconds, the two coaches and both teams were running out to the fallen player, huddling over him, forming a tight, hushed circle around him.

Crying, "Bird! Bird!" Shari leapt off the benches and began running to the circle of horrified onlookers.

Greg started to follow, but stopped when he saw a familiar figure crossing the road, running and waving to him.

"Terry!" Greg cried.

Why was his brother coming to the playground? Why wasn't he at his after-school job at the Dairy Freeze?

"Terry? What's happening?" Greg cried.

Terry stopped, gasping for breath, sweat pouring down his bright red forehead. "I . . . ran . . . all . . . the . . . way," he managed to utter.

"Terry, what's wrong?" A sick feeling crept up from Greg's stomach.

As Terry approached, his face held the same

frightened expression as in the photograph Greg had snapped of him.

The same frightened expression. With the same house behind him across the street.

The photograph had come true. Just as the one of Bird lying on the ground had come true.

Greg's throat suddenly felt like cotton wool. He realized that his knees were trembling.

"Terry, what *is* it?" he managed to cry.

"It's Dad," Terry said, putting a heavy hand on Greg's shoulder.

"Huh? Dad?"

"You've got to come home, Greg. Dad—he's been in a bad accident."

"An accident?" Greg's head spun. Terry's words weren't making any sense to him.

"In the new car," Terry explained, again placing a heavy hand on Greg's trembling shoulder. "The new car is wrecked. Completely wrecked."

"Oh," Greg gasped, feeling weak.

Terry squeezed his shoulder. "Come on. Hurry."

Holding the camera tightly in one hand, Greg started running after his brother.

Reaching the street, he turned back to the playground to see what was happening with Bird.

A large crowd was still huddled round Bird, blocking him from sight.

But—what was that dark shadow behind the benches? Greg wondered.

Someone—someone all in black—was hiding back there.

Watching Greg?

"Come *on*!" Terry urged.

Greg stared hard at the benches. The dark figure drew back out of sight.

"Come *on*, Greg!"

"I'm coming!" Greg shouted, and followed his brother towards their house.

The hospital walls were pale green. The uniforms worn by the nurses scurrying through the brightly lit corridors were white. The floor tiles beneath Greg's feet as he hurried with his brother towards their father's room were dark brown with orange specks.

Colours.

All Greg could see were blurs of colours, indistinct shapes.

His trainers thudded noisily against the hard tile floor. He could barely hear them over the pounding of his heart.

Wrecked. The car had been wrecked.

Just like in the photo.

Greg and Terry turned a corner. The walls in this corridor were pale yellow. Terry's cheeks were red. Two doctors passed by wearing lime-green surgical gloves.

Colours. Only colours.

Greg blinked, tried to see clearly. But it was all

passing by too fast, all too unreal. Even the sharp hospital smell, that unique aroma of stale food, and disinfectant, couldn't make it real for him.

Then the two brothers entered their father's room, and it all became real.

The colours faded. The images became sharp and clear.

Their mother jumped up from the folding chair beside the bed. "Hi, boys." She clenched a wadded-up tissue in her hand. It was obvious that she had been crying. She forced a tight smile on her face, but her eyes were red-rimmed, her cheeks pale and puffy.

Stopping just inside the doorway of the small room, Greg returned his mother's greeting in a soft, choked voice. Then his eyes, focusing clearly now, turned to his father.

Mr Banks had a mummy-like bandage covering his hair. One arm was in a plastercast. The other lay at his side and had a tube attached just below the wrist, dripping a dark liquid into the arm. The bedsheet was pulled up to his chest.

"Hey—how's it going, boys?" their father asked. His voice sounded muffled, as if coming from far away.

"Dad—" Terry started.

"He's going to be okay," Mrs Banks interrupted, seeing the frightened looks on her sons' faces.

187

"I feel great," Mr Banks said groggily.

"You don't *look* so great," Greg blurted out, stepping up cautiously to the bed.

"I'm okay. Really," their father insisted. "A few broken bones. That's all." He sighed, then winced from some pain. "I suppose I'm lucky."

"You're very lucky," Mrs Banks agreed quickly.

What's the lucky part? Greg wondered silently to himself. He couldn't take his eyes off the tube stuck into his father's arm.

Again, he thought of the photograph of the car. It was up in his room at home, tucked into the secret compartment in his headboard.

The photo showing the car wreck, the driver's side caved in.

Should he tell them about it?

He couldn't decide.

Would they believe him if he *did* tell them?

"What'd you break, Dad?" Terry asked, sitting down on the radiator in front of the windowsill, shoving his hands into his jeans pockets.

"Your father broke his arm and a few ribs," Mrs Banks answered quickly. "And he had slight concussion. The doctors are checking him for internal injuries. But, so far, so good."

"I was lucky," Mr Banks repeated. He smiled at Greg.

"Dad, I've got to tell you about this photo I took," Greg said suddenly, speaking rigidly, his

188

voice trembling with nervousness. "I took a picture of the new car, and—"

"The car is completely wrecked," Mrs Banks interrupted. Sitting on the edge of the folding chair, she rubbed her fingers, working her wedding ring round and round, something she always did when she was nervous. "I'm glad you boys didn't see it." Her voice caught in her throat. Then she added, "It's a miracle he wasn't more badly hurt."

"This photo—" Greg started again.

"Later," his mother said brusquely. "Okay?" She gave him a meaningful stare.

Greg felt his face grow hot.

This is *important*, he thought.

Then he decided they probably wouldn't believe him, anyway. Who would believe such a crazy story?

"Will we be able to get another new car?" Terry asked.

Mr Banks nodded carefully. "I have to phone the insurance company," he said.

"I'll phone them when I get home," Mrs Banks said. "You don't exactly have a hand free."

Everyone laughed at that, nervous laughter.

"I feel pretty sleepy," Mr Banks said. His eyes were halfway closed, his voice muffled.

"It's the painkillers the doctors gave you," Mrs Banks told him. She leaned forward and

189

patted his hand. "Get some sleep. I'll come back in a few hours."

She stood up, still fiddling with her wedding ring, and motioned with her head towards the door.

"Bye, Dad," Greg and Terry said in unison.

Their father muttered a reply. They followed their mother out of the door.

"What *happened*?" Terry asked as they made their way past a nurses' office, then down the long, pale yellow corridor. "I mean, the accident."

"Some man went straight through a red light," Mrs Banks said, her red-rimmed eyes staring straight ahead. "He ploughed right into your father's side of the car. Said his brakes weren't working." She shook her head, tears forming in the corners of her eyes. "I don't know," she said, sighing. "I just don't know what to say. Thank goodness he's going to be okay."

They turned into the green corridor, walking side by side. Several people were waiting patiently for the lift at the far side of the corridor.

Once again, Greg found himself thinking of the pictures he had taken with the weird camera.

First Michael. Then Terry. Then Bird. Then his father.

All four photos had shown something terrible. Something terrible that hadn't happened yet.

And then all four photos had come true.

Greg felt a chill as the lift doors opened and the small crowd of people moved forwards to squeeze inside.

What was the truth about the camera? he wondered.

Does the camera *show* the future?

Or does it actually *cause* bad things to happen?

"Yeah. I know Bird's okay," Greg said into the phone receiver. "I saw him yesterday, remember? He was lucky. Really lucky. He didn't have concussion or anything."

On the other end of the line—in the house next door—Shari agreed, then repeated her request.

"No, Shari. I really don't want to," Greg replied vehemently.

"*Bring* it," Shari demanded. "It's *my* birthday."

"I don't want to bring the camera. It's not a good idea. Really," Greg told her.

It was the next weekend. Saturday afternoon. Greg had been nearly out of the door, on his way next door to Shari's birthday party, when the phone rang.

"Hi, Greg. Why aren't you on your way to my party?" Shari had asked after he'd run to pick up the phone.

"Because I'm on the phone to you," Greg had replied drily.

"Well, bring the camera, okay?"

Greg hadn't looked at the camera, hadn't removed it from its hiding place since his father's accident.

"I don't want to bring it," he insisted, despite Shari's high-pitched demands. "Don't you understand, Shari? I don't want anyone else to get hurt."

"Oh, Greg," she said, talking to him as if he were a three-year-old. "You don't really believe that, do you? You don't really believe that the camera can hurt people."

Greg was silent for a moment. "I don't know what I believe," he said finally. "I only know that first Michael, then Bird—"

Greg swallowed hard. "And I had a dream, Shari. Last night."

"Huh? What kind of dream?" Shari asked impatiently.

"It was about the camera. I was taking everyone's photo. My whole family—Mum, Dad, and Terry. They were barbecuing. In the back garden. I held up the camera. I kept saying, 'Say Cheese, Say Cheese', over and over again. And when I looked through the viewfinder, they were smiling back at me—but . . . they were skeletons. All of them. Their skin had gone, and—and . . ."

Greg's voice trailed off.

"What a stupid dream," Shari said, laughing.

"But that's why I don't want to bring the camera," Greg insisted. "I think—"

"Bring it, Greg," she interrupted. "It's not your camera, you know. All four of us were in the Coffman house. It belongs to all four of us. Bring it."

"But *why*, Shari?" Greg demanded.

"It'll be a laugh, that's all. It takes such weird pictures."

"That's for sure," Greg muttered.

"We don't have anything else to do for my party," Shari told him. "I wanted to rent a video, but my mum says we have to go outdoors. She doesn't want her precious house messed up. So I thought we could take everyone's picture with the weird camera. You know. See what strange things come out."

"Shari, I really don't—"

"Bring it," she ordered. And hung up.

Greg stood for a long time staring at the phone receiver, thinking hard, trying to decide what to do.

Then he replaced the receiver and headed reluctantly up to his room.

With a loud sigh, he pulled the camera from its hiding place in his headboard. "It's Shari's birthday, after all," he said aloud to himself.

His hands were trembling as he picked it

up. He realized he was afraid of it.

I shouldn't be doing this, he thought, feeling a tight knot of dread in the pit of his stomach.

I know I shouldn't be doing this.

17

"How's it going, Bird?" Greg called, making his way across the flagstone patio to Shari's back garden.

"I'm feeling okay," Bird said, slapping his friend a high five. "The only problem is, ever since that ball hit me," Bird continued, frowning, "from time to time I start—*pluuccck cluuuck cluuuuuuck*!—clucking like a chicken!" He flapped his arms and started strutting across the back garden, clucking at the top of his voice.

"Hey, Bird—go lay an egg!" someone yelled, and everyone laughed.

"Bird's at it again," Michael said, shaking his head. He gave Greg a friendly punch on the shoulder. Michael, his red hair unbrushed as usual, was wearing faded jeans and a flowered Hawaiian sports shirt about three sizes too big for him.

"*Where*'d you find that shirt?" Greg asked,

holding Michael at arm's length by the shoulders to admire it.

"In a cereal box," Bird chimed in, still flapping his arms.

"My grandmother gave it to me," Michael said, frowning.

"He made it in home economics," Bird interrupted. One joke was never enough.

"But why did you *wear* it?" Greg asked.

Michael shrugged. "Everything else was dirty."

Bird bent down, picked up a small clump of soil from the lawn, and rubbed it on the back of Michael's shirt. "Now this one's dirty, too," he declared.

"Hey, you—" Michael reacted with playful anger, grabbing Bird and shoving him into the hedge.

"Did you bring it?"

Hearing Shari's voice, Greg turned towards the house and saw her jogging across the patio in his direction. Her black hair was pulled back in a single plait, and she had on an oversized, silky yellow top that came down over black lycra leggings.

"Did you bring it?" she repeated eagerly. A charm bracelet filled with tiny silver charms—a birthday present—jangled at her wrist.

"Yeah." Greg reluctantly held up the camera.

"Excellent," she declared.

197

"I really don't want—" Greg started.

"You can take *my* picture first seeing as it's my birthday," Shari interrupted. "Here. How's this?" She struck a sophisticated pose, leaning against a tree with her hand behind her head.

Greg obediently raised the camera. "Are you sure you want me to do this, Shari?"

"Yeah. Come on. I want to take everyone's picture."

"But it'll probably come out weird," Greg protested.

"I know," Shari replied impatiently, holding her pose. "That's the fun of it."

"But, Shari—"

"Michael puked on his shirt," he heard Bird telling someone near the hedge.

"I did not!" Michael was screaming.

"You mean it looks like that *naturally*?" Bird asked.

Greg could hear a lot of raucous laughing, all of it at Michael's expense.

"Will you take the picture!" Shari cried, holding on to the slender trunk of the tree.

Greg pointed the lens at her and pressed the button. The camera whirred, and then the undeveloped, white square rolled out.

"Hey, are we the only boys invited?" Michael asked, walking up to Shari.

"Yeah. Just you three," Shari said. "And nine girls."

"Oh, wow." Michael made a face.

"Take Michael's photo next," Shari told Greg.

"No way!" Michael replied quickly, raising his hands as if to shield himself and backing away. "The last time you took my photograph with that thing, I fell down the stairs."

Trying to get away, Michael backed right into Nina Blake, one of Shari's friends. She reacted with a squeal of surprise, then gave him a playful shove, and he kept right on backing away.

"Michael, come on. It's *my* party," Shari called.

"What are we going to do? Is this *it*?" Nina demanded from halfway across the garden.

"I thought we'd take everyone's photo and then play a game or something," Shari told her.

"A game?" Bird chimed in. "You mean like Spin the Bottle?"

A few kids laughed.

"Truth or Dare!" Nina suggested.

"Yeah. Truth or Dare!" a couple of other girls called in agreement.

"Oh, no," Greg groaned quietly to himself. Truth or Dare meant a lot of kissing and awkward, embarrassing stunts.

Nine girls and only three boys.

It was going to be *really* embarrassing.

How could Shari *do* this to us? he wondered.

"Well, did it come out?" Shari asked, grabbing

his arm. "Let me see."

Greg was so upset about having to play Truth or Dare, he had forgotten about the photo developing in his hand. He held it up, and they both examined it.

"Where am I?" Shari asked in surprise. "What were you aiming at? You missed me!"

"Huh?" Greg stared at the snapshot. There was the tree. But no Shari. "Weird! I pointed it straight at you. I lined it up carefully," he protested.

"Well, you missed me. I'm not in the photo," Shari replied disgustedly.

"But, Shari—"

"I mean, come *on*—I'm not invisible, Greg. I'm not a vampire or something. I can see my reflection in mirrors. And I do usually show up in photos."

"But, look—" Greg stared hard at the photograph. "There's the tree you were leaning against. You can see the trunk clearly. And there's the spot where you were standing."

"But where *am* I?" Shari demanded, jangling her charm bracelet noisily. "Never mind." She grabbed the picture from him and tossed it on the grass. "Take another one. Quick."

"Well, okay. But—" Greg was still puzzling over the photo. Why hadn't Shari shown up in it? He bent down, picked it up, and shoved it into his pocket.

"Stand closer this time," she instructed.

Greg moved a few steps closer, carefully centred Shari in the viewfinder, and snapped the picture. A square of film zipped out of the front.

Shari walked over and pulled the picture from the camera. "This one had better come out," she said, staring hard at it as the colours began to darken and take form.

"If you really want pictures of everyone, we should get another camera," Greg said, his eyes also locked on the snapshot.

"Hey—I don't *believe* it!" Shari cried.

Again, she was invisible.

The tree photographed clearly, in perfect focus. But Shari was nowhere to be seen.

"You were right. The stupid camera is broken," she said disgustedly, handing the photo to Greg. "Forget it." She turned away from him and called to the others. "Hey, boys—Truth or Dare!"

There were some cheers and some groans.

Shari headed them back to the woods behind her back garden to play. "More privacy," she explained. There was a circular clearing just beyond the trees, a perfect, private place.

The game was just as embarrassing as Greg had imagined. Among the boys, only Bird seemed to be enjoying it. Bird loves stupid stuff like this, Greg thought, with some envy.

Luckily, after little more than half an hour, he

heard Mrs Walker, Shari's mum, calling from the house, summoning them back to cut the birthday cake.

"Aw, too bad," Greg said sarcastically. "Just when the game was getting good."

"We have to get out of the woods, anyway," Bird said, grinning. "Michael's shirt is scaring the squirrels."

Laughing and talking about the game, the kids made their way back to the patio where the pink-and-white birthday cake, candles all lit, was waiting on the round patio table.

"I must be a pretty bad mother," Mrs Walker joked, "allowing you all to go off into the woods by yourselves."

Some of the girls laughed.

Cake knife in her hand, Mrs Walker looked around. "Where's Shari?"

Everyone turned their eyes to search the back garden. "She was with us in the woods," Nina told Mrs Walker. "Just a minute ago."

"Hey, Shari!" Bird called, cupping his hands to his mouth as a megaphone. "Earth calling Shari! It's cake time!"

No reply.

No sign of her.

"Did she go into the house?" Greg asked.

Mrs Walker shook her head. "No. She didn't come past the patio. Is she still in the woods?"

"I'll go and check," Bird told her. Calling

Shari's name, he ran to the edge of the trees at the back of the garden. Then he disappeared into the trees, still calling.

A few minutes later, Bird emerged, signalling to the others with a shrug.

No sign of her.

They searched the house. The front garden. The woods again.

But Shari had vanished.

18

Greg sat in the shade with his back against the tree trunk, the camera on the ground at his side, and watched the blue-uniformed policemen.

They covered the back garden and could be seen bending low as they climbed around in the woods. He could hear their voices, but couldn't make out what they were saying. Their faces were intent, bewildered.

More policemen arrived, grim-faced, business-like.

And then, even more dark-uniformed police-men.

Mrs Walker had called her husband home from a golf game. They sat huddled together on canvas chairs in a corner of the patio. They whispered to each other, their eyes darting across the garden. Holding hands, they looked pale and worried.

Everyone else had left.

On the patio, the table was still set. The

birthday candles had burned all the way down, the blue and red wax melting in hard puddles on the pink-and-white icing, the cake untouched.

"No sign of her," a red-cheeked policeman with a white-blond moustache was telling the Walkers. He pulled off his cap and scratched his head, revealing short, blond hair.

"Did someone . . . take her away?" Mr Walker asked, still holding his wife's hand.

"No sign of a struggle," the policeman said. "No sign of anything, really."

Mrs Walker sighed loudly and lowered her head. "I just don't understand it."

There was a long, painful silence.

"We'll keep looking," the policeman said. "I'm sure we'll find . . . something."

He turned and headed towards the woods.

"Oh. Hi." He stopped in front of Greg, staring down at him as if seeing him for the first time. "You still here, son? All the other guests have gone home." He pushed his hair back and replaced his cap.

"Yeah, I know," Greg replied solemnly, lifting the camera into his lap.

"I'm Officer Riddick," he said.

"Yeah, I know," Greg repeated softly.

"How come you didn't go home after we'd talked with you, like the others?" Riddick asked.

"I'm just upset, I suppose," Greg told him. "I mean, Shari's a good friend, you know?" He cleared his throat, which felt dry and tight. "Besides, I live just over there." He gestured with his head to his house next door.

"Well, you might as well go home, son," Riddick said, turning his eyes to the woods with a frown. "This search could take a long time. We haven't found a thing back there yet."

"I know," Greg replied, rubbing his hand against the back of the camera.

And I know that this camera is the reason Shari is missing, he thought, feeling miserable and frightened.

"One minute she was there. The next minute she had gone," the policeman said, studying Greg's face as if looking for answers there.

"Yeah," Greg replied. "It's so weird."

It's weirder than anyone knows, he thought.

The camera made her invisible. The camera did it.

First, she vanished from the photo.

Then she vanished in real life.

The camera did it to her. I don't know how. But it did.

"Do you have something more to tell me?" Riddick asked, hands resting on his hips, his right hand just above the worn brown holster that carried his pistol. "Did you see something? Something that might give us a clue, help us out? Something you didn't remember to tell me before?"

Should I tell him? Greg wondered.

If I tell him about the camera, he'll ask where I got it. And I'll have to tell him that I got it in the Coffman house. And we'll get into trouble for breaking in there.

But—big deal. Shari is missing. Gone. Vanished. That's a lot more important.

I should tell him, Greg decided.

But then he hesitated. If I tell him, he won't believe me.

If I tell him, how will it help bring Shari back?

"You look very troubled," Riddick said, squatting down next to Greg in the shade. "What's your name again?"

"Greg. Greg Banks."

"Well, you look very troubled, Greg," the policeman repeated softly. "Why don't you tell me what's bothering you? Why don't you tell me what's on your mind? I think it'll make you feel a lot better."

Greg took a deep breath and glanced up to the patio. Mrs Walker had covered her face with her hands. Her husband was leaning over her, trying to comfort her.

"Well . . ." Greg started.

"Go ahead, son," Riddick urged softly. "Do you know where Shari is?"

"It's the camera," Greg blurted out. He could suddenly feel the blood throbbing against his temples.

207

He took a deep breath and then continued. "You see, this camera is weird."

"What do you mean?" Riddick asked quietly.

Greg took another deep breath. "I took Shari's photograph. Before. When I first arrived. I took two photos. And she was invisible. In both of them. See?"

Riddick closed his eyes, then opened them. "No. I don't understand."

"Shari was invisible in the photo. Everything else was there. But she wasn't. She had vanished, see. And, then, later, she vanished for real. The camera—it predicts the future, I think. Or it makes bad things happen." Greg raised the camera, attempting to hand it to the policeman.

Riddick made no attempt to take it. He just stared hard at Greg, his eyes narrowing, his expression hardening.

Greg felt a sudden stab of fear.

Oh, no, he thought. Why is he looking at me like that?

What is he going to do?

Greg continued to hold the camera out to the policeman.

But Riddick quickly climbed to his feet. "The camera makes bad things happen?" His eyes burned into Greg's.

"Yes," Greg told him. "It isn't my camera, see? And every time I take a photo—"

"Son, that's enough," Riddick said gently. He reached down and rested a hand on Greg's trembling shoulder. "I think you're very upset, Greg," he said, his voice almost a whisper. "I don't blame you. This is very upsetting for everyone."

"But it's *true*—" Greg began to insist.

"I'm going to ask that officer over there," Riddick said, pointing, "to take you home now. And I'm going to ask him to tell your parents that you've been through a very frightening experience."

I *knew* he wouldn't believe me, Greg thought angrily.

How could I have been so stupid?

Now he thinks I'm some kind of a nut case.

Riddick called to a policeman at the side of the house near the hedge.

"No, that's okay," Greg said, quickly pulling himself up, cradling the camera in his hand. "I can make it home okay."

Riddick eyed him suspiciously. "You sure?"

"Yeah. I can walk by myself."

"If you have anything to tell me later," Riddick said, lowering his gaze to the camera, "just call the station, okay?"

"Okay," Greg replied, walking slowly towards the front of the house.

"Don't worry, Greg. We'll do our best," Riddick called after him. "We'll find her. Put the camera away and try to get some rest, okay?"

"Okay," Greg muttered.

He hurried past the Walkers, who were still huddled together under the parasol on the patio.

Why was I so stupid? he asked himself as he walked home. Why did I expect that policeman to believe such a weird story?

I'm not even sure I believe it myself.

A few minutes later, he pulled open the back door and entered his kitchen. "Anybody home?"

No reply.

He headed through the back hall towards the living room. "Anyone home?"

No one.

Terry was at work. His mother must be visiting his dad at the hospital.

Greg felt depressed. He really didn't feel like being alone now. He really wanted to tell them about what had happened to Shari. He really wanted to talk to them.

Still cradling the camera, he climbed the stairs to his room.

He stopped in the doorway, blinked twice, then uttered a cry of horror.

His books were scattered all over the floor. The covers had been pulled off his bed. His desk drawers were all open, their contents strewn around the room. The desk lamp was on its side on the floor. All of his clothes had been pulled from the chest of drawers and his wardrobe and tossed everywhere.

Someone had been in Greg's room—and had turned it upside down!

Who would do this? Greg asked himself, staring in horror at his ransacked room.

Who would tear my room apart like this?

He realized that he knew the answer. He knew who would do it, who *had* done it.

Someone looking for the camera.

Someone desperate to get the camera back.

Spidey?

The creepy man who dressed all in black was living in the Coffman house. Was he the owner of the camera?

Yes, Greg knew, Spidey had done it.

Spidey had been watching Greg, spying on Greg from behind the benches at the Little League game.

He knew that Greg had his camera. *And he knew where Greg lived.*

That thought was the most chilling of all.

He knew where Greg lived.

Greg turned away from the chaos in his room,

leaned against the wall of the hallway, and closed his eyes.

He pictured Spidey, the dark figure creeping along so evilly on his spindly legs. He pictured him inside the house, Greg's house. Inside Greg's room.

He was here, thought Greg. He pawed through all my things. He wrecked my room.

Greg stepped back into his room. He felt all mixed up. He felt like shouting angrily and crying for help all at once.

But he was all alone. No one to hear him. No one to help him.

What now? he wondered. What now?

Suddenly, leaning against the doorframe, staring at his ransacked room, he knew what he had to do.

"Hey, Bird, it's me."

Greg held the receiver in one hand and wiped the sweat off his forehead with the other. He'd never worked so hard—or so fast—in all his life.

"Did they find Shari?" Bird asked eagerly.

"I haven't heard. I don't think so," Greg said, his eyes surveying his room. Almost back to normal.

He had put everything back, cleaned and straightened. His parents would never guess.

"Listen, Bird, I'm not calling about that," Greg said, speaking rapidly into the phone. "Phone Michael for me, okay? Meet me at the playground. By the baseball pitch."

"When? Now?" Bird asked, sounding confused.

"Yeah," Greg told him. "We have to meet. It's important."

"It's almost dinnertime," Bird protested. "I don't know if my parents—"

214

"It's important," Greg repeated impatiently. "I've got to see you both. Okay?"

"Well . . . maybe I can sneak out for a few minutes," Bird said, lowering his voice. And then Greg heard him shout to his mother. "It's no one, Ma! I'm talking to no one!"

Boy, *that's* quick thinking! Greg thought sarcastically. He's a worse liar than I am!

And then he heard Bird call to his mum! "I *know* I'm on the phone. But I'm not talking to anyone. It's only Greg."

Thanks a lot, pal, Greg thought.

"I gotta go," Bird said.

"Get Michael, okay?" Greg urged.

"Yeah. Okay. See you." He hung up.

Greg replaced the receiver, then listened for his mother. Silence downstairs. She still wasn't home. She didn't know about Shari, Greg realized. He knew she and his dad were going to be very upset.

Very upset.

Almost as upset as he was.

Thinking about his missing friend, he went to his bedroom window and looked down on her garden next door. It was deserted now.

The policemen had all left. Shari's shaken parents must have gone inside.

A squirrel sat under the wide shade of the big tree, gnawing furiously at an acorn, another acorn at his feet.

In the corner of the window, Greg could see the birthday cake, still sitting forlornly on the deserted table, the places all set, the decorations still standing.

A birthday party for ghosts.

Greg shuddered.

"Shari is alive," he said aloud. "They'll find her. She's alive."

He knew what he had to do now.

Forcing himself away from the window, he hurried to meet his two friends.

22

"No way," Bird said heatedly, leaning against the bench. "Have you gone totally bananas?"

Swinging the camera by its cord, Greg turned hopefully to Michael. But Michael avoided Greg's stare. "I'm with Bird," he said, his eyes on the camera.

Since it was just about dinnertime, the playground was nearly deserted. A few little kids were on the swings at the other end. Two kids were riding their bikes round and round the playing field.

"I thought maybe you two would come with me," Greg said, disappointed. He kicked up a clump of grass with his trainer. "I have to return this thing," he continued, raising the camera. "I know it's what I have to do. I have to put it back where I found it."

"No way," Bird repeated, shaking his head. "I'm not going back to the Coffman house. Once was enough."

"Chicken?" Greg asked angrily.

"Yeah," Bird quickly admitted.

"You don't have to take it back," Michael argued. He pulled himself up the side of the benches, climbed onto the third deck of seats, then lowered himself to the ground.

"What do you mean?" Greg asked impatiently, kicking at the grass.

"Just dump it, Greg," Michael urged, making a throwing motion with one hand. "Chuck it. Throw it away somewhere."

"Yeah. Or leave it right here," Bird suggested. He reached for the camera. "Give it to me. I'll hide it under the seats."

"You don't understand," Greg said, swinging the camera out of Bird's reach. "Throwing it away won't do any good."

"Why not?" Bird asked, making another swipe for the camera.

"Spidey'll just come back for it," Greg told him heatedly. "He'll come back to my room looking for it. He'll come after me. I know it."

"But what if we get caught taking it back?" Michael asked.

"Yeah. What if Spidey's there in the Coffman house, and he catches us?" Bird said.

"You don't understand," Greg cried. "He knows where I live! He was in my house. He was in my *room*! He wants his camera back, and—"

"Here. Give it to me," Bird said. "We don't have to go back to that house. He can find it. Right here."

He grabbed again for the camera.

Greg held tightly to the strap and tried to tug it away.

But Bird grabbed the side of the camera.

"No!" Greg cried out as it flashed. And whirred.

A square of film slid out.

"No!" Greg cried to Bird, horrified, staring at the white square as it started to develop. "You took *my* picture!"

His hand trembling, he pulled the photo from the camera.

What would it show?

"Sorry," Bird said. "I didn't mean to—"

Before he could finish his sentence, a voice interrupted from behind the benches. "Hey—what've you got there?"

Greg looked up from the developing photograph in surprise. Two tough-looking boys stepped out of the shadows, their expressions hard, their eyes on the camera.

He recognized them immediately—Joey Ferris and Mickey Ward—two ninth-graders who hung around together, always swaggering around, acting tough, picking on kids younger than them.

Their speciality was taking kids' bikes, riding off on them, and dumping them somewhere. There was a rumour going around school that Mickey had once beaten up a kid so badly that the kid was crippled for life. But Greg believed Mickey had made up that rumour and spread it himself.

Both boys were big for their age. Neither of them did very well at school. And even though they were always stealing bikes and skateboards, and terrorizing little kids, and getting into fights, neither of them ever seemed to get into serious trouble.

Joey had short blond hair, slicked straight up, and wore a diamond-like stud in one ear. Mickey had a round, red face full of pimples, stringy black hair down to his shoulders, and was working a toothpick between his teeth. Both boys were wearing heavy T-shirts and jeans.

"Hey, I've gotta get home," Bird said quickly, half-stepping, half-dancing away from the benches.

"Me, too," Michael said, unable to keep the fear from showing on his face.

Greg tucked the photo into his jeans pocket.

"Hey, you found my camera," Joey said, grabbing it out of Greg's hand. His small, grey eyes burned into Greg's as if searching for a reaction. "Thanks, man."

"Give it back, Joey," Greg said with a sigh.

"Yeah. Don't take that camera," Mickey told his friend, a smile spreading over his round face. "It's *mine!*" He wrestled the camera away from Joey.

"Give it back," Greg insisted angrily, reaching out his hand. Then he softened his tone. "Come on. It isn't mine."

221

"I *know* it isn't yours," Mickey said, grinning. "Because it's *mine!*"

"I have to give it back to the owner," Greg told him, trying not to whine, but hearing his voice edge up.

"No, you don't. I'm the owner now," Mickey insisted.

"Haven't you ever heard of finders keepers?" Joey asked, leaning over Greg menacingly. He was about six inches taller than Greg, and a lot more muscular.

"Hey, let him have the thing," Michael whispered in Greg's ear. "You wanted to get rid of it—right?"

"No!" Greg protested.

"What's your problem, Freckle Face?" Joey asked Michael, eyeing Michael up and down.

"No problem," Michael said meekly.

"Hey—say cheese!" Mickey aimed the camera at Joey.

"Don't do it," Bird interrupted, waving his hands frantically.

"Why not?" Joey demanded.

"Because your face will break the camera," Bird said, laughing.

"You're really funny," Joey said sarcastically, narrowing his eyes threateningly, hardening his features. "You want that stupid smile to be permanent?" He raised a big fist.

"I know this kid," Mickey told Joey, pointing

at Bird. "Thinks he's hot stuff."

Both boys stared hard at Bird, trying to scare him.

Bird swallowed hard. He took a step back, bumping into the benches. "No, I don't," he said softly. "I don't think I'm hot stuff."

"He looks like something I stepped in yesterday," Joey said.

He and Mickey cracked up, laughing high-pitched hyena laughs and slapping each other high fives.

"Listen, you two. I really need the camera back," Greg said, reaching out a hand to take it. "It isn't any good, anyway. It's broken. And it doesn't belong to me."

"Yeah, that's right. It's broken," Michael added, nodding his head.

"Yeah. Right," Mickey said sarcastically. "Let's just see." He raised the camera again and pointed it at Joey.

"Really. I need it back," Greg said desperately.

If they took a picture with the camera, Greg realized, they might discover its secret. That its pictures showed the future, showed only bad things happening to people. That the camera was evil. Maybe it even *caused* evil.

"Say cheese," Mickey instructed Joey.

"Just snap the stupid thing!" Joey replied impatiently.

No, Greg thought. I can't let this happen. I've got to return the camera to the Coffman house, to Spidey.

Impulsively, Greg leapt forward. With a cry, he snatched the camera away from Mickey's face.

"Hey—" Mickey reacted in surprise.

"Let's *go!*" Greg shouted to Bird and Michael.

And without another word, the three friends turned and began running across the deserted playground towards their homes.

His heart thudding in his chest, Greg gripped the camera tightly and ran as fast as he could, his trainers pounding over the dry grass.

They're going to catch us, Greg thought, panting loudly now as he raced towards the street. They're going to catch us and pound us. They're going to take back the camera. We're dead meat. Dead meat.

Greg and his friends didn't turn round until they were across the street. Breathing noisily, they looked back—and cried out in relieved surprise.

Joey and Mickey hadn't budged from beside the benches. They hadn't chased after them. They were leaning against the benches, laughing.

"Catch you later, boys!" Joey called after them.

"Yeah. Later," Mickey repeated.

They both burst out laughing again, as if they had said something hilarious.

"That was close," Michael said, still breathing hard.

"They mean it," Bird said, looking very troubled. "They'll catch us later. We're history."

"Tough talk. They're just a lot of hot air," Greg insisted.

"Oh, yeah?" Michael cried. "Then why did we run like that?"

"Because we're late for dinner," Bird joked. "See you two. I'm gonna get it if I don't hurry."

"But the camera—" Greg protested, still gripping it tightly in one hand.

"It's too late," Michael said, nervously raking a hand back through his red hair.

"Yeah. We'll have to do it tomorrow or something," Bird agreed.

"Then you'll come with me?" Greg asked eagerly.

"Uh . . . I've gotta go," Bird said without answering.

"Me, too," Michael said quickly, avoiding Greg's stare.

All three of them turned their eyes back to the playground. Joey and Mickey had disappeared. Probably off to terrorize some other kids.

"Later," Bird said, slapping Greg on the shoulder as he headed away. The three friends split up, running in different directions across

225

lawns and drives, heading home.

Greg had run all the way to his front garden before he remembered the photograph he had shoved into his jeans pocket.

He stopped in the drive and pulled it out.

The sun was lowering behind the garage. He held the photo up close to his face to see it clearly.

"Oh, no!" he cried. "I don't believe it!"

"This is *impossible!*" Greg cried aloud, gaping at the photograph in his trembling hand.

How had Shari got into the photo?

It had been taken a few minutes before, in front of the benches on the playground.

But there was Shari, standing close beside Greg.

His hand trembling, his mouth hanging open in disbelief, Greg goggled at the photo.

It was very clear, very sharp. There they were on the playground. He could see the baseball pitch in the background.

And there they were. Greg and Shari.

Shari standing so clear, so sharp—right next to him.

And they were both staring straight ahead, their eyes wide, their mouths open, their expressions frozen in horror as a large shadow covered them both.

"Shari?" Greg cried, lowering the snapshot

and darting his eyes over the front garden. "Are you here? Can you hear me?"

He listened.

Silence.

He tried again.

"Shari? Are you here?"

"Greg!" a voice called.

Uttering a startled cry, Greg spun around. "Huh?"

"Greg!" the voice repeated. It took him a while to realize that it was his mother, calling to him from the front door.

"Oh. Hi, Mum." Feeling dazed, he slid the photo back into his jeans pocket.

"Where've you been?" his mother asked as he made his way to the door. "I heard about Shari. I've been so upset. I didn't know where you were."

"Sorry, Mum," Greg said, kissing her on the cheek. "I—I should've left a note."

He stepped into the house, feeling strange and out-of-sorts, sad and confused and frightened, all at the same time.

Two days later, on a day of high, grey clouds, the air hot and smoggy, Greg paced back and forth in his room after school.

The house was empty except for him. Terry had gone off a few hours before to his after-school job at the Dairy Freeze. Mrs Banks had driven to the hospital to pick up Greg's dad, who was finally coming home.

Greg knew he should be happy about his dad's return. But there were still too many things troubling him, tugging at his mind.

Frightening him.

For one thing, Shari still hadn't been found.

The police were completely baffled. Their new theory was that she'd been kidnapped.

Her frantic, grieving parents waited at home by the phone. But no kidnappers phoned to demand a ransom.

There were no clues of any kind.

Nothing to do but wait. And hope.

As the days passed, Greg felt more and more guilty. He was sure Shari hadn't been kidnapped. He knew that somehow, the camera had made her disappear.

But he couldn't tell anyone else what he believed.

No one would believe him. Anyone he tried to tell the story to would think he was crazy.

Cameras can't be evil, after all.

Cameras can't make people fall down stairs. Or crash their cars.

Or vanish from sight.

Cameras can only record what they see.

Greg stared out of his window, pressing his forehead against the glass, looking down on Shari's back garden. "Shari—where *are* you?"

he asked aloud, staring at the tree where she had posed.

The camera was still hidden in the secret compartment in his headboard. Neither Bird nor Michael would agree to help Greg return it to the Coffman house.

Besides, Greg had decided to hold on to it a while longer, in case he needed it as proof.

In case he decided to confide his fears about it to someone.

In case . . .

His other fear was that Spidey would come back, back to Greg's room, back for the camera.

So much to be frightened about.

He pushed himself away from the window. He had spent so much time in the past couple of days staring down at Shari's empty back garden.

Thinking. Thinking.

With a sigh, he reached into the headboard and pulled out two of the pictures he had hidden in there along with the camera.

The two photos were the ones taken the past Saturday at Shari's party. Holding one in each hand, Greg stared at them, hoping he could see something new, something he hadn't noticed before.

But the photos hadn't changed. They still showed her tree, her back garden, green in the sunlight. And no Shari. No one where Shari had been standing. As if the lens had penetrated right through her.

Staring at the photos, Greg let out a cry of anguish.

If only he had never gone into the Coffman house.

If only he had never stolen the camera.

If only he had never taken any photos with it.

If only . . . if only . . . if only . . .

Before he realized what he was doing, he was ripping the two photos into tiny pieces.

Panting loudly, his chest heaving, he tore at the pictures and let the pieces fall to the floor.

When he had ripped them both into tiny shreds of paper, he flung himself facedown on his bed and closed his eyes, waiting for his heart to stop pounding, waiting for the heavy feeling of guilt and horror to lift.

Two hours later, the phone by his bed rang.

It was Shari.

"Shari—is it really you?" Greg shouted into the phone.

"Yeah. It's me!" She sounded as surprised as he did.

"But how? I mean—" His mind was racing. He didn't know what to say.

"Your guess is as good as mine," Shari told him. And then she said, "Hold on a minute." And he heard her step away from the phone to talk to her mother. "Mum—stop crying, okay. Mum—it's really me. I'm home."

A few seconds later, she came back on the line. "I've been home for two hours, and Mum's still crying and carrying on."

"I feel like crying, too," Greg admitted. "I—I just can't believe it! Shari, where *were* you?"

The line was silent for a long moment. "I don't know," she answered finally.

"Huh?"

"I really don't. It was just so weird, Greg. One

minute, there I was at my birthday party. The next minute, I was standing in front of my house. And it was two days later. But I don't remember being away. Or being anywhere else. I don't remember anything at all."

"You don't remember going away? Or coming back?" Greg asked.

"No. Nothing," Shari said, her voice trembling.

"Shari, those pictures I took of you—remember? With the weird camera? You were invisible in them—"

"And then I disappeared," she said, finishing his thought.

"Shari, do you think—?"

"I don't know," she replied quickly. "I—I have to get off the phone now. The police are here. They want to question me. What am I going to tell them? They're going to think I had amnesia or blacked out or something."

"I—I don't know," Greg said, completely bewildered. "We have to talk. The camera—"

"I can't now," she told him. "Maybe tomorrow. Okay?" She called to her mother that she was coming. "Bye, Greg. See you." And then she hung up.

Greg replaced the receiver, but sat on the edge of his bed staring at the phone for a long time.

Shari was back.

She'd been back for about two hours.

Two hours. Two hours. Two hours.

He turned his eyes to the clock radio beside the phone.

Just two hours before, he had ripped up the two photos of an invisible Shari.

His mind whirred with wild ideas, insane ideas.

Had he brought Shari back by ripping up the photos?

Did this mean that the camera had *caused* her to disappear? That the camera had *caused* all of the terrible things that showed up in its photographs?

Greg stared at the phone for a long time, thinking hard.

He knew what he had to do. He had to talk to Shari. And he had to return the camera.

He met Shari in the playground the next afternoon. The sun floated high in a cloudless sky. Eight or nine kids were engaged in a noisy brawl of a soccer game, running one way, then the other across the outfield of the baseball diamond.

"Hey—you look like *you!*" Greg exclaimed as Shari came jogging up to where he stood beside the benches. He pinched her arm. "Yeah. It's you, okay."

She didn't smile. "I feel fine," she told him, rubbing her arm. "Just confused. And tired. The police asked me questions for hours. And when they finally went away, my parents started up."

"Sorry," Greg said quietly, staring down at his trainers.

"I think Mum and Dad believe that somehow it's my fault that I disappeared," Shari said, resting her back against the side of the benches, shaking her head.

"It's the camera's fault," Greg muttered. He raised his eyes to hers. "The camera is evil."

Shari shrugged. "Maybe. I don't know what to think. I really don't."

He showed her the photo, the one showing the two of them in the playground staring in horror as a shadow crept over them.

"How weird," Shari exclaimed, studying it hard.

"I want to take the camera back to the Coffman house," Greg said heatedly. "I can go home and get it now. Will you help me? Will you come with me?"

Shari started to reply, but stopped.

They both saw the dark shadow move, sliding towards them quickly, silently, over the grass.

And then they saw the man dressed all in black, his spindly legs pumping hard as he came at them.

Spidey!

Greg grabbed Shari's hand, frozen in fear.

He and Shari gasped in terror as Spidey's slithering shadow crept over them.

Greg had a shudder of recognition. He knew the photograph had just come true.

As the dark figure of Spidey moved towards them like a black tarantula, Greg pulled Shari's hand. "Run!" he cried in a shrill voice he didn't recognize.

He didn't have to say it. They were both running now, gasping as they ran across the grass towards the street. Their trainers thudded loudly on the ground as they reached the pavement and kept running.

Greg turned to see Spidey closing the gap. "He's catching up!" he managed to cry to Shari, who was a few steps ahead of him.

Spidey, his face still hidden in the shadows of his black baseball cap, moved with startling speed, his long legs kicking high as he pursued them.

"He's going to catch us!" Greg cried, feeling as if his chest were about to burst. "He's ... too ... fast!"

Spidey moved even closer, his shadow scuttling over the grass.

Closer.

When the car horn honked, Greg screamed.

He and Shari stopped short.

The horn blasted out again.

Greg turned to see a familiar young man inside a small hatchback. It was Jerry Norman, who lived across the street. Jerry lowered his car window. "Is this man chasing you?" he asked excitedly. Without waiting for an answer, he backed the car towards Spidey. "I'm calling the cops, mister!"

Spidey didn't reply. Instead, he turned and darted across the street.

"I'm warning you—" Jerry called after him.

But Spidey had disappeared behind a tall hedge.

"Are you kids okay?" Greg's neighbour demanded.

"Yeah. Fine," Greg managed to reply, still breathing hard, his chest heaving.

"We're okay. Thanks, Jerry," Shari said.

"I've seen that man around the neighbourhood," the young man said, staring through the windscreen at the tall hedge. "Never thought he was dangerous. You kids want me to call the police?"

"No. It's okay," Greg replied.

As soon as I give him back his camera, he'll

238

stop chasing us, Greg thought.

"Well, be careful—okay?" Jerry said. "You need a lift home or anything?" He studied their faces as if trying to determine how frightened and upset they were.

Greg and Shari both shook their heads. "We'll be okay," Greg said. "Thanks."

Jerry warned them once again to be careful, then drove off, his tyres squealing as he turned the corner.

"That was close," Shari said, her eyes on the hedge. "Why was Spidey chasing us?"

"He thought I had the camera. He wants it back," Greg told her. "Meet me tomorrow, okay? In front of the Coffman house. Help me put it back?"

Shari stared at him without replying, her expression thoughtful, wary.

"We're going to be in danger—all of us—until we put that camera back," Greg insisted.

"Okay," Shari said quietly. "Tomorrow."

27

Something scurried through the tall weeds of the unmowed front lawn. "What *was* that?" Shari cried, whispering even though no one else was in sight. "It was too big to be a squirrel."

She lingered behind Greg, who stopped to look up at the Coffman house. "Maybe it was a racoon or something," Greg told her. He gripped the camera tightly in both hands.

It was a little after three o'clock the next afternoon, a hazy, overcast day. Mountains of dark clouds threatening rain were rolling across the sky, stretching behind the house, bathing it in shadow.

"It's going to storm," Shari said, staying close behind Greg. "Let's get this over with and go home."

"Good idea," he said, glancing up at the heavy sky.

Thunder rumbled in the distance, a low roar. The old trees that dotted the front garden whispered and shook.

"We can't just run inside," Greg told her, watching the sky darken. "First we've got to make sure Spidey isn't there."

Making their way quickly through the tall grass and weeds, they stopped at the living room window and peered in. Thunder rumbled, low and long, in the distance. Greg thought he saw another creature scuttle through the weeds around the corner of the house.

"It's too dark in there. I can't see a thing," Shari complained.

"Let's check out the basement," Greg suggested. "That's where Spidey hangs out, remember?"

The sky darkened to an eerie grey-green as they made their way to the back of the house and dropped to their knees to peer down through the basement windows at ground level.

Squinting through the dust-covered windowpanes they could see the makeshift, plywood table Spidey had made, the wardrobe against the wall, its doors still open, the colourful, old clothing spilling out, the empty frozen food boxes scattered on the floor.

"No sign of him," Greg whispered, cradling the camera in his arm as if it might try to escape from him if he didn't hold it tightly. "Let's get moving."

"Are—are you sure?" Shari stammered. She

wanted to be brave. But the thought that she had disappeared for two days—completely *vanished*, most likely because of the camera—that frightening thought lingered in her mind.

Michael and Bird were chicken, she thought. But maybe they were the clever ones.

She wished this were over. All over.

A few seconds later, Greg and Shari pushed open the front door. They stepped into the darkness of the front hall. And stopped.

And listened.

And then they both jumped at the sound of the loud, sudden crash directly behind them.

28

Shari was the first to regain her voice. "It's just the door!" she cried. "The wind—"

A gust of wind had made the front door slam.

"Let's get this over with," Greg whispered, badly shaken.

"We never should've broken into this house in the first place," Shari whispered as they made their way on tiptoe, step by creaking step, down the dark hallway towards the basement stairs.

"It's a little late for that," Greg replied sharply.

Pulling open the door to the basement steps, he stopped again. "What's that banging sound upstairs?"

Shari's features tightened in fear as she heard it too, a repeated, almost rhythmic banging.

"Shutters?" Greg suggested.

"Yeah," she agreed quickly, breathing a sigh of relief. "A lot of the shutters are loose, remember?"

The whole house seemed to groan.

Thunder rumbled outside, closer now.

They stepped onto the landing, then waited for their eyes to adjust to the darkness.

"Couldn't we just leave the camera up here, and run?" Shari asked, more of a plea than a question.

"No. I want to put it back," Greg insisted.

"But, Greg—" She tugged at his arm as he started down the stairs.

"No!" He pulled out of her grasp. "He was in my *room*, Shari! He tore everything apart, looking for it. I want him to find it where it belongs. If he doesn't find it, he'll come back to my house. I *know* he will!"

"Okay, okay. Let's just hurry."

It was brighter in the basement, grey light seeping down from the four ground-level windows. Outside, the wind swirled and pushed against the windowpanes. A pale flash of lightning made shadows flicker against the basement wall. The old house groaned as if unhappy about the storm.

"What was *that*? Footsteps?" Shari stopped halfway across the basement and listened.

"It's just the house," Greg insisted. But his quivering voice revealed that he was as frightened as his companion, and he stopped to listen, too.

Bang. Bang. Bang.

The shutter high above them continued its rhythmic pounding.

"Where did you find the camera, anyway?" Shari whispered, following Greg to the far wall opposite the enormous boiler with its cobwebbed ducts sprouting up like pale tree limbs.

"Over here," Greg told her. He stepped up to the worktable and reached for the vice clamped on the edge. "When I turned the vice, a door opened up. Some kind of hidden shelf. That's where the camera—"

He cranked the handle of the vice.

Once again, the door to the secret shelf popped open.

"Good," he whispered excitedly. He flashed Shari a smile.

He shoved the camera onto the shelf, tucking the carrying strap under it. Then he pushed the door closed. "We're out of here."

He felt so much better. So relieved. So much *lighter*.

The house groaned and creaked. Greg didn't care.

Another flash of lightning, brighter this time, like a camera flash, sent shadows flickering on the wall.

"Come on," he whispered. But Shari was already ahead of him, making her way carefully over the empty food cartons strewn everywhere, hurrying towards the steps.

245

They were halfway up the stairs, Greg one step behind Shari, when, above them, Spidey stepped silently into view on the landing, blocking their escape.

Greg blinked and shook his head, as if he could shake away the image of the figure that stared darkly down at him.

"No!" Shari cried out, and fell back against Greg.

He grabbed for the railing, forgetting that it had fallen under Michael's weight during their first unfortunate visit to the house. Luckily, Shari regained her balance before toppling them both down the stairs.

Lightning flashed behind them, sending a flash of white light across the staircase. But the unmoving figure on the landing above them remained shrouded in darkness.

"Let us go!" Greg finally managed to cry, finding his voice.

"Yeah. We've brought back your camera!" Shari added, sounding shrill and frightened.

Spidey didn't reply. Instead, he took a step towards them, onto the first step. And then he descended another step.

Nearly stumbling again, Greg and Shari backed down to the basement floor.

The wooden stairs squeaked in protest as the dark figure stepped slowly, steadily, down. As he reached the basement floor, a crackling bolt of lightning cast a blue light over him, and Greg and Shari saw his face for the first time.

In the brief flash of colour, they saw that he was old, older than they had imagined. That his eyes were small and round like dark marbles. That his mouth was small, too, pursed in a tight, menacing grimace.

"We returned the camera," Shari said, staring in fear as Spidey crept closer. "Can't we go now? Please?"

"Let me see," Spidey said. His voice was younger than his face, warmer than his eyes. "Come."

They hesitated. But he gave them no choice.

Ushering them back across the cluttered floor to the worktable, he wrapped his large, spidery hand over the vice and turned the handle. The door opened. He pulled out the camera and held it close to his face to examine it.

"You shouldn't have taken it," he told them, speaking softly, turning the camera in his hands.

"We're sorry," Shari said quickly.

"Can we go now?" Greg asked, edging towards the stairs.

"It's not an ordinary camera," Spidey said, raising his small eyes to them.

"We know," Greg blurted out. "The pictures it took. They—"

Spidey's eyes grew wide, his expression angry. "You took pictures with it?"

"Just a few," Greg told him, wishing he had kept his mouth shut. "They didn't come out. Really."

"You know about the camera, then," Spidey said, moving quickly to the middle of the floor.

Was he trying to block their escape? Greg wondered.

"It's broken or something," Greg said uncertainly, shoving his hands into his jeans pockets.

"It's not broken," the tall, dark figure said softly. "It's evil." He motioned towards the low plywood table. "Sit there."

Shari and Greg exchanged glances. Then, reluctantly, they sat down on the edge of the board, sitting stiffly, nervously, their eyes darting towards the staircase, towards escape.

"The camera is evil," Spidey repeated, standing over them, holding the camera in both hands. "I should know. I helped to create it."

"You're an inventor?" Greg asked, glancing at Shari, who was nervously tugging at a strand of her black hair.

"I'm a scientist," Spidey replied. "Or, I should

say, I *was* a scientist. My name is Fredericks. Dr Fritz Fredericks." He transferred the camera from one hand to the other. "My lab partner invented this camera. It was his pride and joy. More than that, it would have made him a fortune. *Would* have, I say." He paused, a thoughtful expression sinking over his face.

"What happened to him? Did he die?" Shari asked, still fiddling with the strand of hair.

Dr Fredericks sniggered. "No. Worse. I stole the invention from him. I stole the plans and the camera. I was evil, you see. I was young and greedy. So very greedy. And I wasn't above stealing to make my fortune."

He paused, eyeing them both as if waiting for them to say something, to offer their disapproval of him, perhaps. But when Greg and Shari remained silent, staring up at him from the low plywood table, he continued his story.

"When I stole the camera, it caught my partner by surprise. Unfortunately, from then on, all of the surprises were mine." A strange, sad smile twisted across his aged face. "My partner, you see, was much more evil than I was."

Dr Fredericks coughed into his hand then began to pace in front of Greg and Shari as he talked, speaking softly, slowly, as if remembering the story for the first time in a long while.

"My partner was a *true* evil one. He dabbled in

250

black magic. I should correct myself. He didn't just dabble. He was quite a master of it all."

He held up the camera, waving it above his head, then lowering it. "My partner put a curse on the camera. If he couldn't profit from it, he wanted to make sure that I never would, either. And so he put a curse on it."

He turned his gaze on Greg, leaning over him. "Do you know about how some primitive peoples fear the camera? They fear the camera because they believe that if it takes their picture, it will steal their soul." He patted the camera. "Well, this camera really *does* steal souls."

Staring up at the camera, Greg shuddered.

The camera had stolen Shari away.

Would it have stolen *all* of their souls?

"People have died because of this camera," Dr Fredericks said, uttering a slow, sad sigh. "People close to me. That's how I came to learn of the curse, to learn of the camera's evil. And then I learned something just as frightening—the camera cannot be destroyed."

He coughed, cleared his throat noisily, and began to pace in front of them again. "And so I vowed to keep the camera a secret. To keep it away from people so it cannot do its evil. I lost my job. My family. I lost everything because of it. But I am determined to keep the camera where it can do no harm."

251

He stopped pacing with his back towards them. He stood silently, shoulders hunched, lost in thought.

Greg quickly climbed to his feet and motioned for Shari to do the same. "Well . . . uh . . . I suppose it's good we returned it," he said hesitantly. "Sorry we caused so much trouble."

"Yeah, we're very sorry," Shari repeated sincerely. "It's back in the right hands now."

"Goodbye," Greg said, starting towards the steps. "It's getting late, and we—"

"No!" Dr Fredericks shouted, startling them both. He moved quickly to block the way. "I'm afraid you can't go. You know too much."

"I can never let you leave," Dr Fredericks said, his face flickering in the blue glow of a lightning flash. He crossed his bony arms in front of his black sweatshirt.

"But we won't tell anyone," Greg said, his voice rising until the words became a plea. "Really."

"Your secret is safe with us," Shari insisted, her frightened eyes on Greg.

Dr Fredericks stared at them menacingly, but didn't reply.

"You can trust us," Greg said, his voice quivering. He cast a frightened glance at Shari.

"Besides," Shari said, "even if we *did* tell anyone, who would believe us?"

"Enough talk," Dr Fredericks snapped. "It won't do you any good. I've worked too long and too hard to keep the camera a secret."

A rush of wind pushed against the windows, sending up a low howl. The wind carried a drum roll of rain. The sky through the basement windows was as black as night.

"You—can't keep us here *forever!*" Shari cried, unable to keep the growing terror from her voice.

The rain pounded against the windows now, a steady downpour.

Dr Fredericks drew himself up straight. He seemed to grow taller. His tiny eyes burned into Shari's. "I'm so sorry," he said, his voice a whisper of regret. "So sorry. But I have no choice."

He took another step towards them.

Greg and Shari exchanged frightened glances. From where they stood, in front of the low plywood table in the middle of the basement, the steps seemed a hundred miles away.

"Wh-what are you going to do?" Greg cried, shouting over a burst of thunder that rattled the basement windows.

"Please—!" Shari begged. "Don't—!"

Dr Fredericks moved forward with surprising speed. Holding the camera in one hand, he grabbed Greg's shoulder with the other.

"No!" Greg screamed. "Let go!"

"Let go of him!" Shari screamed.

She suddenly realized that both of Dr Fredericks' hands were occupied.

This may be my only chance, she thought.

She took a deep breath and lunged forward.

Dr Fredericks' eyes bulged, and he cried out in

surprise as Shari grabbed the camera with both hands and pulled it away from him. He made a frantic grab for the camera, and Greg burst free.

Before the desperate man could take another step, Shari raised the camera to her eye and pointed the lens at him.

"Please—no! Don't push the button!" the old man cried.

He lurched forward, his eyes wild, and grabbed the camera with both hands.

Greg stared in horror as Shari and Dr Fredericks grappled, both holding onto the camera, each trying desperately to wrestle it away from the other.

FLASH!

The bright burst of light startled them all.

Shari grabbed the camera. "Run!" she screamed.

The basement became a whirring blur of greys and blacks as Greg hurled himself towards the stairs.

He and Shari ran side by side, slipping over the food cartons, jumping over tin cans and empty bottles.

Rain thundered against the windows. The wind howled, pushing against the glass. They could hear Dr Fredericks' anguished screams behind them.

"Did it take our picture or his?" Shari asked.

"I don't know. Just *hurry*!" Greg screamed.

The old man was howling like a wounded animal, his cries competing with the rain and wind pushing at the windows.

The stairs weren't that far away. But it seemed to take forever to reach them.

Forever.

Forever, Greg thought. Dr Fredericks wanted to keep Shari and him down there *forever*.

Panting loudly, they both reached the dark staircase. A deafening clap of thunder made them stop and turn round.

"Huh?" Greg cried aloud.

To his shock, Dr Fredericks hadn't chased after them.

And his anguished cries had stopped.

The basement was silent.

"What's going on?" Shari cried breathlessly.

Squinting back into the darkness, it took Greg a while to realize that the dark, rumpled form lying on the floor in front of the worktable was Dr Fredericks.

"What happened?" Shari cried, her chest heaving as she struggled to catch her breath. Still clinging to the camera strap, she gaped in surprise at the old man's still body, sprawled on its back on the floor.

"I don't know," Greg replied in a breathless whisper.

Reluctantly, Greg started back towards Dr Fredericks. Following close behind, Shari uttered a low cry of horror when she clearly saw the fallen man's face.

Eyes bulged out, the mouth open in a twisted O of terror, the face stared up at them. Frozen. Dead.

Dr Fredericks was dead.

"What—*happened*?" Shari finally managed to say, swallowing hard, forcing herself to turn away from the ghastly, tortured face.

"I think he died of fright," Greg replied, squeezing her shoulder and not even realizing it.

"Huh? Fright?"

"He knew better than anyone what the camera could do," Greg said. "When you snapped his picture, I think . . . I think it scared him to *death*!"

"I only wanted to throw him off-guard," Shari cried. "I only wanted to give us a chance to escape. I didn't think—"

"The picture," Greg interrupted. "Let's see the picture."

Shari raised the camera. The photo was still half-inside the camera. Greg pulled it out with a trembling hand. He held it up so they could both see it.

"Wow," he exclaimed quietly. "Wow."

The photo showed Dr Fredericks lying on the floor, his eyes bulging, his mouth frozen open in horror.

Dr Fredericks' fright, Greg realized—the fright that had killed him—was there, frozen on film, frozen on his face.

The camera had claimed another victim. This time, forever.

"What do we do now?" Shari asked, staring down at the figure sprawled at their feet.

"First, I'm putting this camera back," Greg said, taking it from her and shoving it back on its shelf. He turned the vice handle, and the door

258

to the secret compartment closed.

Greg breathed a sigh of relief. Hiding the dreadful camera away made him feel so much better.

"Now, let's go home and call the police," he said.

Two days later, a cool, bright day with a gentle breeze rustling the trees, the four friends stopped at the kerb, leaning on their bikes, and stared up at the Coffman house. Even in bright sunlight, the old trees that surrounded the house covered it in shade.

"So you didn't tell the police about the camera?" Bird asked, staring up at the dark, empty front window.

"No. They wouldn't believe it," Greg told him. "Besides, the camera should stay locked up forever. *Forever*! I hope no one ever finds out about it."

"We told the police we ran into the house to get out of the rain," Shari added. "And we said we started to explore while we waited for the storm to blow over. And we found the body in the basement."

"What did Spidey die of?" Michael asked, gazing up at the house.

"The police said it was heart failure," Greg told him. "But we know the truth."

"Wow. I can't believe an old camera could do

so much evil," Bird said.

"I believe it," Greg said quietly.

"Let's get out of here," Michael urged. He put his trainers on the pedals and started to roll away. "This place really creeps me out."

The other three followed, pedalling away in thoughtful silence.

They had turned the corner and were heading up the next road when two figures emerged from the back door of the Coffman house. Joey Ferris and Mickey Ward stepped over the weed-choked lawn onto the drive.

"Those jerks aren't too bright," Joey told his companion. "They never even saw us the other day. Never saw us watching them through the basement window."

Mickey laughed. "Yeah. They're jerks."

"They couldn't hide this camera from *us*. No way, man," Joey said. He raised the camera and examined it.

"Take my picture," Mickey demanded. "Come on. Let's try it out."

"Yeah. Okay." Joey raised the viewfinder to his eye. "Say cheese."

A click. A flash. A whirring sound.

Joey pulled the photo from the camera, and both boys eagerly huddled around it, waiting to see what developed.

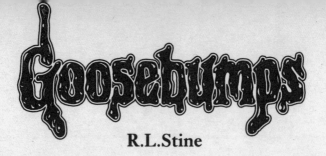

Goosebumps

R.L. Stine

Reader beware, you're in for a scare!

These terrifying tales will send shivers up your spine:

Goosebumps

Reader beware – here's THREE TIMES the scare!

Look out for these bumper GOOSEBUMPS editions. With three spine-tingling stories by R.L. Stine in each book, get ready for three times the thrill … three times the scare … three times the GOOSEBUMPS!